Praise for Lucian Barnes

DESTINED FOR DARKNESS - "Gruesome and intriguing, mixed with the awkwardness of real life!"

—R&M Fab Reviews

DESTINED FOR DARKNESS - "Are you looking for a read that will creep you out and give you nightmares? Destined for Darkness did that for me. In this book, we get a look into the Mancini family. We see how the darkness starts to creep in and eventually take over the lives of first, Frank, and then his son, George. The story shows us how the two men can be seemingly harmless, but hide an evil so vile that even they are repulsed by their own actions.

Despite the fact that this book gave me a major case of the creeps, I was compelled to read on about the horrific things the Mancini men did. I think a writer has done their job well when you are reading and making gagging noises because you can envision the carnage. When you cringe because you can almost see what's going to happen next. If this were a movie, I would have had my hands over my eyes for most of it. Job well done, Mr. Barnes. You thoroughly disturbed me with this book."

—Mindy Nabors, Paranormal Tendencies

DESOLACE - "Chilling, spine-tingling, and other-worldy! Author Lucian Barnes captivates your inner curiosity which compels you to keep on reading. Desolace takes the reader on a whirlwind spin from the real world we know, of serial killers and grisly crime to a dark, fantasy world of enslavement and robotic takeover. A cliff hanger, leaving the reader to wonder if there is more to come and if all the unanswered questions will finally be answered. Will the serial killer, dubbed "the headhunter" ever be caught? Will Julie, his most recent abductee be found, ALIVE?!…or in pieces? DESOLACE, book one, in a series of books by Author Lucian Barnes in his continuing saga of murder, time portals, and an underworld preparing for world domination!"

—RAM Book Reviews

HAVEN - "A strong heroine, awesome narration, unique voice, and vivid dialogue make this book the "perfect" read.

After the first few chapters, the stage is set for a rip-roaring supernatural thriller that will keep you anxiously turning the pages. Our heroine, Katie hunts for Julie and will stop at nothing. Katie dives into a supernatural world that kept me glued to my kindle screen for hours. This author delivers an adrenaline pumping thriller and spellbinding tale with vampires and werewolves that will leave you howling for more. And I won't even get into the 'bugs'! Especially beetles!

I really enjoyed the main character, Katie. The author creates a distinct world for the reader filled with mind-blowing scenes, mystery, and a colorful mix of characters.

This thriller totally held my attention. I can't wait to read the next book! I give this book 5 stars without a doubt and will definitely read more from this talented author."

—Donna Johnson, Author

Cemetery Hill
By
Lucian Barnes

This book is a work of fiction. Names, characters, places, and incidents are products of the author's imagination or are used fictitiously. Any resemblance to actual events or locales or persons, living or dead, is entirely coincidental.

Copyright © 2014 by Lucian Barnes

All rights reserved, including the right to reproduce this book or portions thereof in any form whatsoever.

ISBN: 978-1495906435

Cover art copyright © 2014 by Katie Cowan

Printed in the U.S.A.

This book is dedicated to the memory of my childhood friend, Kevin Welsh, who was taken from the world in his early twenties by Cystic Fibrosis. I cherished every moment we were able to spend together in the short time we had, and even years later you have remained firmly entrenched in my thoughts. One day, we will be reunited in the hereafter to continue our journey of friendship. Until we meet again, my friend. Cheers.

In honor of my fallen friend, and everyone else suffering with Cystic Fibrosis around the world, I have pledged to donate 10% of all royalties I receive from this book, to the Cystic Fibrosis Foundation.

Cemetery Hill

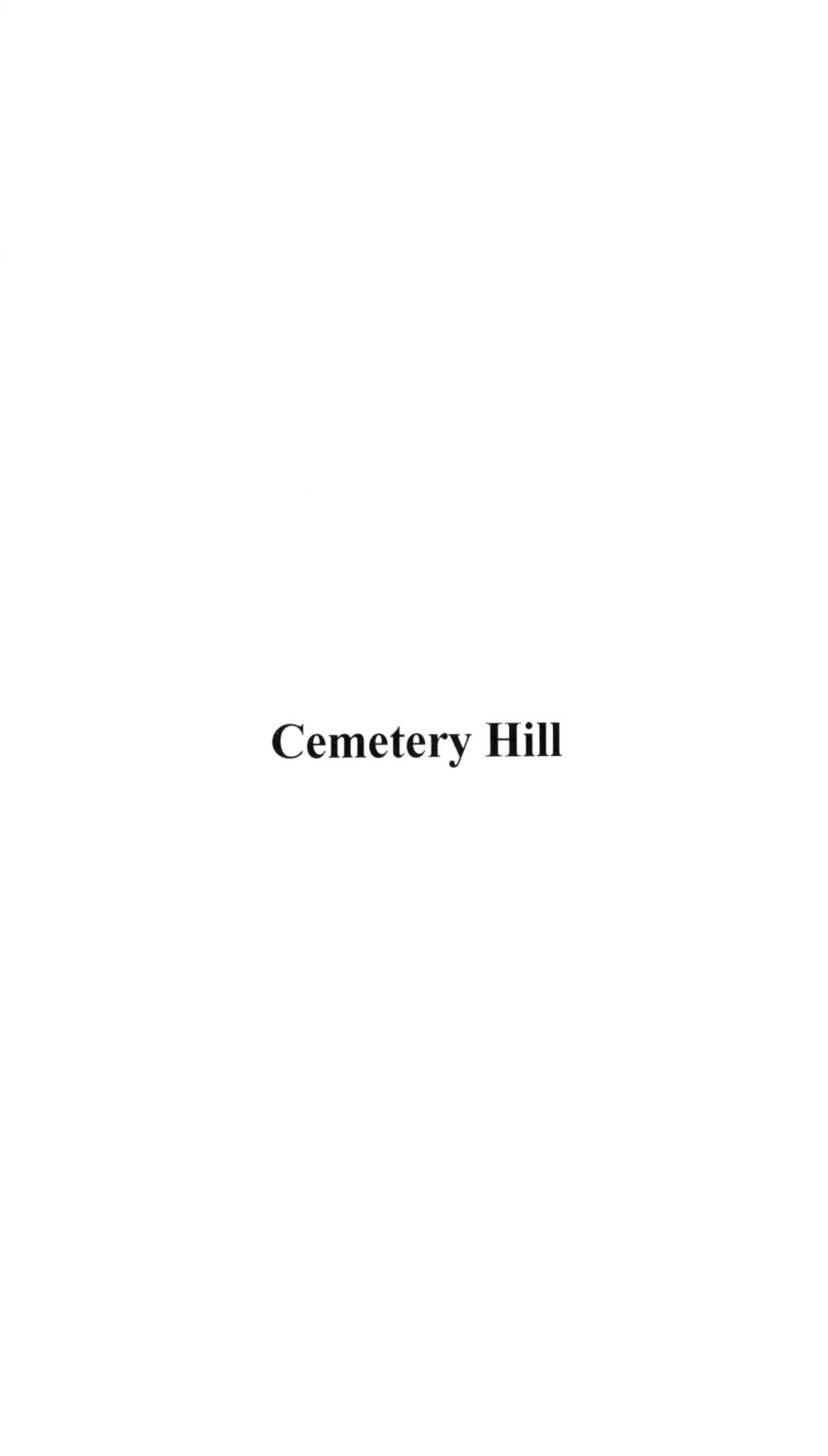

Introduction

Up until now, in the Desolace series, we have gotten our first look at the serial killer known as The Headhunter. He is likely the most terrifying individual you have ever encountered; a prime example of what true evil really is. He abducts, tortures, and maims his victims, keeping their heads as gruesome trophies. Then he taunts the police by leaving the headless corpses of his victims displayed for the entire world to see.

Two high school seniors find out about him after fooling around with an Ouija board one night, accidentally contacting a real spirit; the ghost of one of his victims. The apparition leads Katie and Julie through the woods to show them her killer and the girls make a startling discovery. They recognize the man as their school bus driver.

A strange entity enters the picture, introducing itself to the killer as the Black Knight. He enlists the aid of The Headhunter, bringing him through a portal into the parallel world of Desolace.

He awakens in this new world and is instructed by the Black Knight to abduct people to work in a place known as The Factory. Doing the Black Knight's bidding, his resentment grows every time he restrains himself from killing.

Back on Earth, Katie has what she believes to be a

dream. In this vision she meets a tall, pale sorcerer that calls himself Edward the White. He begs for her assistance, citing the fact that evil has gained entrance to his world from her own and he needs her help to vanquish it.

When Katie awakens, the shimmering spirit that led her to discover the identity of The Headhunter is in her room, beckoning for Katie to follow her once more. She follows, stepping through a portal into what she thought was a dream world.

As she meets the sorcerer who appeared in her "dream" for the first time, he informs Katie that they must form a group of people, comprised solely of individuals from Earth. The only catch? They must all have talents which are unique within the group. This group will consist of: a magician, hunter, warrior, healer, and some type of religious person.

After speaking with Edward at length, Katie soon realizes there is a possibility that her friend, Julie, has been brought to this world. She agrees to help him for the time being; in return she asks for his assistance finding her friend.

Edward agrees to help Katie and they soon set off on their quest. During their travels, they encounter many strange creatures, the likes of which Katie had before considered myth. They also come across more portals that lead to Earth, each seemingly associated with different points in time. They discover that each portal leads them to a specific individual, one whom they will need to form the rest of their group.

After entering a strange telephone booth, the group

finds themselves transported to a future version of Earth; one decimated by an unknown virus which has turned nearly every living soul into a zombie. When Katie realizes they have come out of the portal and landed in the Upper Peninsula of Michigan, she suggests the group head south, hoping to find a way out of this new hell back at her childhood home in Misty Hollows, Ohio.

Along their journey the group is forced to fight for their very lives against the never-ending tide of the undead, but near Detroit they find the final piece of their group, a red-haired former priest studying the ways of the shaman. Shortly thereafter the group encounters a southern man, fleeing to the north to escape the stench of death and the zombie hordes, hoping to find Canada more hospitable.

The group convinces this man, Chris, to give them a ride to Ohio, and after a terrifying ordeal they finally locate an active portal back to Desolace hidden in the Headhunter's old killing grounds. They fight their way through the zombie hordes to get to the portal, only to find themselves in yet another dilemma. Edward's home town of Elysia has come under attack. As he and his ragged team of adventurers race against time to thwart the invasion, the city's lone surviving elder, Jonas, sends them on a mission to the south to locate the Throne of the Gods in hopes of enlisting the aid of the immortal beings.

They find themselves entrenched in battle with a formidable army of cyborgs shortly after leaving Elysia, but manage to emerge victorious only to find the war was just beginning. Stumbling across a deserted town, which seemed to be forgotten by time, Edward is ambushed by a legion of the Black Knight's demonic minions. Barely managing to survive the attack, the group took shelter in an abandoned inn to rest and lick their wounds. As the shroud of night falls over the town, the story continues ...

Chapter 1

The blaring of an air horn as a semi blew past the driveway startled the Black Knight for a moment as he hid in the shadows of the forest near the road across the street from a rambling farmhouse. As he watched, a younger version of his once faithful servant, George, picked up a rolled paper from the grass.

The young man mounted the steps of his porch and walked through the front door, allowing the screen to slam shut behind him. *I need to find a way to convince him to come back to Desolace with me, but I don't want to frighten him away with my appearance. I need a disguise.* He grinned, thoughtfully scratching his chin.

As the Black Knight considered crossing the street to peer through a window to study the younger version of his wayward disciple, a small child burst through the front door, running into the yard. The screen swung open a few seconds later and an attractive, dark-haired woman stepped onto the porch. The child immediately dove into the tall grass as if playing hide-and-seek. "Cassie," the woman yelled, cupping her hands around her mouth. When the child didn't come out of hiding, the woman put her fingers to her lips and let out a shrill, ear-piercing whistle. "Come inside, Cassie. It's time for dinner!"

Reluctantly, the small girl stood up. "Do I gotta? I wanna play for a little bit," she whined.

"Well, if you want to go trick or treating when it gets dark you need to come inside and eat," her mother chided. As if she had uttered the magic words, Cassie skipped clumsily toward the house with a big grin on her face.

"I really get to go this year?" she asked excitedly.

Her mom laughed. "After dinner."

"Yay!" Cassie quickly disappeared back into the house.

"Make sure you wash your hands," the woman shouted after her.

Tearing through the hallway downstairs, Cassie nearly plowed George over as he carried a plate of burgers from the kitchen to the dining room. "Whoa! Slow down," he scolded, barely managing to keep the tray of food from spilling all over the floor.

Impatiently, the Black Knight waited at the edge of the forest across the street from the house, hoping with nightfall he would be able to get closer to the home without drawing attention to himself.

As the sun sank behind the trees, casting long shadows across the lawn in front of the house, he began to hear the voices of small children heading his way. Shrinking back into the woods, he peered around the trunk of a maple to see a group of approximately ten kids, all wearing masks and costumes of one sort or another, stop at the end of George's driveway with pillowcases clutched in their hands.

"That guy is creepy," one of the children dressed like a clown told the others. "I say we keep going."

"Brady's a chicken, Brady's a chicken," a little girl

wearing a fairy costume teased.

"I wanna go up there and see if Cassie can come with us," another girl, painted up by her parents to look like a porcelain doll, pleaded.

All of them except for Brady agreed with her, responding to the plea with an emphatic, "Let's get some candyyyy!"

The girl in the fairy costume took one last look at Brady, who wasn't budging, and chased after her friends.

Kicking at the gravel alongside the road, he looked at the kids who always seemed to tease him about one thing or another and silently wished something would happen to them. *It would serve them right if that guy chopped them into tiny pieces and ate them. They are all poopheads anyway!*

"Brady," a voice whispered from somewhere nearby in the shadows.

"Who ... who's there?" Brady whimpered, looking nervously around him and suddenly wishing he'd stayed with the other children. With no streetlights in the area, the only light came from the porch where all the other kids were clustered awaiting their treats.

"Brady," the voice beckoned to him again, this time sounding closer.

"D-d-don't come any closer," he stammered as his bladder let go, releasing a warm flood of urine down his leg. "I'll scream."

"I don't think you'll have time for that," the Black Knight hissed, his hot, foul breath caressing the boy's face. He could hear the child's teeth chattering in fear as he reached out with one clawed hand, picking the boy up by his throat. Snapping his neck like it were nothing more than a twig, the Black Knight sunk his long teeth into Brady's throat as his head lolled to one side and drank his fill of the warm blood.

Taking the costume off of the boy's limp body, the Black Knight set it aside before heaving the tiny corpse into the woods where he'd been hiding. Shrinking himself down to a suitable size, he donned the costume and approached the house, pretending to be Brady. By the time he made it to the steps leading onto the porch the other children were walking away. Giggles and whispers passed among them. "Look! The little chicken decided to grow a pair after all."

Playing the part, the Black Knight watched the other children scamper off on their way to the next house, leaving who they thought to be Brady alone once again. Turning toward the screen door, he held out the pillowcase to the woman, seeing his target wandering down the hallway behind her.

"Do you need to use the bathroom?" she inquired as politely as she could manage, wrinkling her nose at the smell of urine coming from the child.

"Yes, please," the Black Knight replied, mimicking Brady's voice.

Opening the door, the woman stepped aside. "It's right down the hall," she pointed. "George! Can you show this little boy where the bathroom is, please? I need to go upstairs and see if Cassie is ready."

George poked his head back into the hallway to see the boy dressed as a clown walking toward him as his wife, Jen, disappeared up the stairs. "Right here, little man." He grinned, opening the door for the youngster.

As the boy went inside, George waved a hand in front of his face then returned to the dining room to clear the dinner plates. *Someone needs to give that kid a bath, he stinks! Bad!*

Just as he finished cleaning up the dishes, George heard footsteps on the staircase. Peeking his head around the corner he saw Jen and Cassie entering the hallway coming toward him.

"Don't you look adorable?" He grinned, seeing his daughter in her princess costume carrying a small plastic pumpkin in one hand and a glittery wand in the other.

"Are you gonna come too, Daddy?" Cassie ran to him and hugged George tightly, her bright blue eyes looking up at his face and pleading with him.

"Sorry, honey. I have a lot of stuff to get done tonight," he apologized, giving her a fake, pouty face. He hated to make up excuses like that, but ever since he blew out his knee on a construction site his joints had given him grief every time the weather changed. Spring and fall always seemed to be the worst seasons for him.

It was amazing how quickly children forgot disappointment. Cassie pecked him on the cheek and ran back down the hall to her mom. "I'm ready," she announced excitedly. "Let's go, let's go!"

"We'll be back in a little bit," Jen hollered over her shoulder.

"Bring me back some candy," he shouted at their backs as they walked through the door.

Once they were gone, George looked curiously at the bathroom, wondering if the little boy was still in there.

Walking over to the closed door, he knocked lightly. "Are you still in there, buddy?" Putting his ear to the wood, he couldn't hear any sound coming from the other side. Softly, he rapped again. "Are you okay? Do you need some help getting your costume back on?"

When only silence greeted his questions, George decided to open the door. Turning the knob, it creaked loudly. As the panel swung open it revealed an empty room. Poking his head inside to make sure the boy wasn't hiding, he clicked off the light. *I don't remember seeing him come out*, he thought, scratching his head.

Now that Jen and Cassie were gone, he wandered to the living room, which he considered to be his study, still pondering the disappearance of the young boy. Strolling over to the elaborate floor to ceiling bookshelf he had created during the summer before he met Jen, George reached for one of the books and tilted it backward. The panel slid to the side noiselessly, revealing a stone staircase he'd added during a flurry of home modifications intended to keep his dark side a secret from the outside world.

Stepping into the space behind the bookcase, he flicked a switch on the wall to turn on the lights and send the shelf back to its original position. *Jen would freak the fuck out if she knew about this place,* he thought, grinning as he made his way to the basement.

Arriving at the bottom of the stairs, he opened the heavy steel door in front of him, which he had installed to eliminate any sound from reaching other parts of the house. As he stepped onto the concrete floor of the secret chamber, he flipped the switch set into the wall, turning on a single, bare light bulb dangling from the ceiling.

Muffled cries escaped the nude woman, chained in place to a ring bolted into the floor, who resembled a girl that had rejected him in high school as dim light filtered through her blindfold. Walking closer, George appraised her body by running his rough hands over her naked flesh, causing her bladder to release as she trembled in fear.

"Don't worry, my dear," he whispered softly into her ear. "It will all be over soon."

"George," a voice hissed from behind him.

Startled, he spun around to locate the owner of the voice, angered that someone had dared violate his private place. "Who's there?" he shouted, not seeing anyone at first.

"I have a special job for you." Stepping partially out of the darkened corner was a tall, shadowy shape wearing a clown mask on its face. It kind of resembled the rubber thing he'd seen the boy wearing earlier, but was different somehow, more elongated, as if it were stretched over a larger face.

"That still doesn't tell me who you are!" he growled, his face growing hot as he quickly strode across the room as if he intended to kill the intruder for his trespass.

When George got to within a few feet of the Black Knight, the eyes within the mask began to emanate a fierce, yellow glow. The face of the clown stretched further, and long, jagged teeth became visible through the mouth hole of the mask, causing George to freeze in terror. "What the fuck are you, man?"

The Black Knight cackled with insane laughter. "If you decide to obey my will I could be your best friend," he cooed, "but if you defy me ... well, let's just say it wouldn't be a wise decision on your part."

"Obey your will? What do you want from me?"

"In time I will show you what your purpose will be, but for now you have to do something for me to show you will be loyal and do what I command." The Black Knight's eyes gleamed with new hope.

"And what might that be?" George inquired nervously.

"History has a way of repeating itself, does it not? You've done this before and for us to move forward you must do it again. Kill your family."

Chapter 2

Shaking his head as if he were trying to dispel an illusion, Edward glanced up at the female silhouette standing in the doorway. "Mother?" He couldn't begin to comprehend why she would be here, provided it was truly her and not a hallucination of the most comforting image he could conjure up. The light of the dying fire outside gave off just enough light for him to see Katie's shadowed figure standing next to the older woman.

"Edward? Is that really you?" Her voice crackled unsteadily as she spoke. George drifted just beneath the surface of Victoria's consciousness, allowing the woman to come forward, knowing it would make the exchange of pleasantries more believable. He didn't give up complete control, however, paranoid that she would warn Edward of his intrusion.

Sliding his chair backwards and attempting to stand, Edward wobbled like a drunk for a few seconds then crumpled to the floor in a heap before Katie could cross the room to help prevent his fall. His embarrassment was temporarily masked by the grimace of pain etched across his face as Edward looked up to see Katie rushing toward him.

"Something isn't right," Brian announced, suddenly appearing in the doorway behind Victoria as Katie helped Edward to regain his feet. It was difficult to tell if there was any reaction at all to his announcement, the darkened interior of the inn masking the features of everyone inside. "Even though the threat of the tiny, demonic creatures seems to have passed, I can still sense something evil lurking very nearby," he began again when no one responded to his first proclamation.

Startled by the voice behind him, George turned Victoria's head to regard Brian, trying to assess if the red-haired man was aware of his presence. Moving forward briefly to take control, unwilling to risk the old woman betraying him, George caused her body to tremble slightly to give the impression of fear when he locked eyes with the shaman. "What is wrong with your eyes, young man?" Waiting for Brian to respond, a shaky hand touched Victoria's shoulder.

"Don't be alarmed, Mother," Edward whispered reassuringly. "Though it may seem unusual, maybe even terrifying, his eyes glazing over like that is the closest thing we have to an early warning system. More often than not, it serves to alert us of potential danger."

Turning her head toward the sound of her son's voice, she attempted a weak smile. Her quivering lips made it obvious that his words did nothing to soothe her fear. Seeing her son up close for the first time in a week didn't help to quell her nervousness either. "You look like death," she gasped.

After everything he had been through today, Edward was surprised he had managed to survive. "I've had better days." He chuckled, bending down to plant a kiss on her cheek. "If it weren't for the amazing friends I have surrounded myself with, I may have perished in battle."

Following the brief conversation, her eyes flitting between Edward, his mother, and Brian, Katie began to get the vibe that something wasn't as it should be. There appeared to be something just beyond her grasp going on, like an unformed word resting on the tip of her tongue. Suddenly, it came to her, like a blinking neon sign. "I hate to interrupt, but something is really bothering me and I need to ask." Turning her penetrating gaze toward Victoria, Katie spoke her mind. "Why are you out here in no-man's land instead of resting safely behind the castle walls of Elysia?"

The question shocked Edward. In his delirious state, he hadn't even considered why his mother was here. Briefly, he recalled a conversation with Jonas regarding his mom. The elder had been concerned about her mental health, citing incidences which occurred recently where Victoria hadn't seemed to be herself. When the initial confusion passed, he turned back to face the old woman. "She has a point, Mother. You should be tucked away in your bed in the safety of the castle, not wandering through the countryside unescorted. The world outside of Elysia is a very dangerous place, and not someplace you should be traveling by yourself," Edward scolded vehemently.

"It's safer outside the city," Victoria retorted angrily. "After you left, legions of mechanical creatures assaulted Elysia. The town is nothing more than a gigantic pile of rubble now. Every person who called Elysia their home has fled to outlying areas." Victoria paused for a moment, taking a deep breath before going on. "If I were to venture a guess, I would say at least half of them didn't make it out of the city alive!"

Katie's tenuous grip on Edward wasn't enough to keep him upright after his mother's words struck home. He sank to the floor as if he had been sucker punched in the gut, his mouth gaping open in disbelief. After leaving Elysia and encountering the large force of cyborgs, Edward thought they had thwarted the impending attack on his home town. However, if what his mother said was true, there must have been a contingent that flanked them in the darkness. He didn't want to think his opponent had outwitted him, but her words were evidence that his supposed victory a few nights ago had likely been nothing more than a diversion. "I think I am going to be sick," he mumbled sadly.

Gathering her resolve, Katie wiped the tears from her eyes and crouched down beside Edward. Throwing her arms around him in what she hoped would be a comforting hug, she whispered in his ear, "I'm sure that nothing I say at this point will help to ease your pain, but you had to know something like this could happen. Why else would Jonas have summoned you back to Elysia and sent you on this mission?"

Turning to face her, his own tears threatening to spill down his cheeks, he nodded. "You're probably right. Jonas had a vision of the downfall of Elysia. I'm sure a combination of that vision, and the small incursion afterward, was what prompted him to summon me. I just don't understand why he stayed behind if he knew it would mean his death."

"I'm sure he had his reasons, Edward. He was probably just trying to keep you focused on the mission, likely he knew you would be worried and distracted if he told you everything he saw in his vision."

Edward remained quiet for a moment, silently contemplating how much more he could endure. "I don't think I should be the one to lead us anymore," he blurted, his voice hitching with emotion.

After his declaration, the entire inn seemed to gasp. "Have you lost your mind? There is no one better suited to the task," Katie murmured, her crouched legs buckling beneath the enormity of Edward's confession and causing her to sink to the floor completely.

Turning Victoria's head to the side, George grinned with delight. *This is going to be like taking candy from a baby,* he thought.

"In my opinion, any one of you would be a more appropriate leader. The only thing I seem to be proficient at is delivering us into the arms of the enemy," Edward countered sadly. "If things keep going the way they have been, there won't be any of us left by the time we reach the Throne of the Gods."

"Well, that's your opinion," Katie protested. "I doubt there is a single person among us that feels the way you do." In the dim light filtering through the doorway, she looked from face to face for confirmation. Each met her gaze with a nod of agreement. "See what I mean?" She took hold of Edward's chin, which was hanging down and nearly touching his chest, and raised it so he could see the reaction of the others.

Edward let out a weary sigh. "At least all of you have faith in me. I just hope it's not misplaced," he mumbled, his voice laden with despair.

The conflagration outside of the inn burned itself out within an hour or two of the conclusion of their heated leadership debate. Amber had still not returned, leaving the group to wonder if she had abandoned them. The lone bright spot of the evening had been Victoria. Apparently she had visited this town in the past and was somewhat familiar with the layout of the inn. As such, she was able to guide each of them to rooms containing beds, even in total darkness.

As Katie lay on one of the straw mattresses, her fingers laced together behind her head, she stared toward the ceiling even though the room was pitch black. The earlier conversation with Edward was weighing heavily on her mind, and she couldn't help the thoughts swirling through her head. *In theory, Edward has rarely led us into danger. It was, more often than not, Amber who we were following. Edward might have been giving the commands, but Amber was the one guiding us.*

Letting out an exasperated sigh, she tried to keep her hopes alive, praying that when morning came Edward would be his old self. Even if it were a beaten and tattered version of the man she had come to respect, it would certainly be preferable to the broken man she had witnessed earlier. One who now seemed to doubt his every move and his worthiness to be their leader.

Chapter 3

The clouds of the previous day had vanished like a bad memory, allowing the morning sunlight to pierce the dust-covered windows of the inn. Feeling the warmth on his flesh, Edward rubbed his hands over his face. Cracking an eye open he sat up quickly, startled fully awake by the unfamiliar surroundings. Grimacing in pain, he pushed himself up from the bed and walked to the room's only window. Brushing away the thick coating of grime on its surface, he peered outside. When he saw his horse, lying dead in the street below, the realization of where he was struck him like a club to the back of his head. Turning away, Edward strolled back to the straw mattress and sat down heavily, closing his eyes and taking a deep, calming breath.

Hearing a scraping noise, grinding softly like a wooden chair being lightly dragged across the planked floor, his head whipped around toward the sound. When he didn't immediately locate the source, Edward leaned toward the foot of the bed, and sighed with relief. It was only Jack. *He must have shifted the stump Katie lashed to his body.* It made Edward smile, knowing that in his weakened condition his friend had stood guard to make sure nothing happened to him during the night.

The previous evening's conversation wasn't much more than a hazy blur in his mind, but he did recall bits and pieces of it. He remembered being depressed and feeling unworthy of the group's devotion to him. Nonetheless, it was a new day now, and his tortured mind rested easier, knowing that no matter how he felt … the world around him had not come to an end while he slept. A thin smile crept across his face as he rose from the bed to check on the others.

Jack awoke immediately when he heard Edward's booted feet shuffling toward the door. Stretching his limbs for a moment, he stood up and hobbled into the hallway after him.

The first couple of doors Edward came to were open, revealing nothing more than empty beds, dust, and more cobwebs than you could shake a stick at. Coming to the end of the hall, he stopped near the partially open threshold and knocked lightly. Hearing the mumbling of a female voice he pushed it open further, revealing Katie sitting cross-legged on the bed. "Good morning." He smiled, but his grin evaporated when she looked him in the eyes. Noticing her haggard appearance, he had to ask, "Did you sleep at all?"

"I don't think so, but I might have nodded off here and there," she admitted with a thin smile that looked more like a grimace. "You seem to be in a better mood than last night." Straightening her legs, Katie scooted to the edge of the bed and stood.

"The miracles of a good night's slumber," he remarked as she crossed the room and hugged him.

"I'm glad. I hated to see you so down on yourself." She yawned. "I know your wounds need more time to heal properly, but it might be a good idea to get everyone together so we can figure out our next move."

"As much as I don't want to admit it, you are probably right about my needing to rest a while longer before attempting to tackle our mission fully. I agree that we need to work out what lies ahead for us, even if my remaining behind for a day or two is part of that equation," he conceded.

"Well, as you've probably noticed, I've been up all night thinking. I have a few ideas to toss around." Katie's lips parted in a crooked, half-smile.

"Once we get everyone else together, I would be happy to hear them." He winked.

Victoria had disappeared at some point during the night. Brian had informed them before they retired last night that he would stand guard, but while he was doing everything he could to keep his friends safe he must have nodded off for a short time. "I never saw, heard, or felt anything out of place after everyone went to bed last night." He shrugged, actually feeling relieved that Edward's mother had slipped past him during the night. Something wasn't right about her, but nobody other than him seemed to notice the difference. Not that he knew her well enough to be able to distinguish normal behavior in her mannerisms. It was just a gut feeling. One which seemed in tune with his inner radar for evil. He glanced across the table at Edward, then Katie, to judge their reactions to his revelation.

Katie sat with a vacant look on her face as if it were a chalkboard that someone had erased, making Brian wonder if she was sleeping with her eyes open. Edward, on the other hand, seemed thoroughly distraught. The conflicting emotions flickering across his features appeared to drift between worry, confusion, and fear. Almost as if his mind was riddled with several different voices, arguing amongst each other like Edward had a split personality disorder. Brian snapped his fingers in front of the wizard's face, as if attempting to wake his friend from a trance. Edward's eyes slowly began to focus and show signs of alertness.

Turning his gaze toward the floor, Edward looked for any indication of a possible struggle. Seeing nothing to suggest that his mother had been abducted while they slept, he glanced back toward Brian. "From what I can tell, she must have left on her own accord," he stated in disbelief. "Why would she do such a thing?"

"Don't take this the wrong way ..." Brian started, his eyebrows knitted together in worry, fearing the reaction he was likely to provoke if he spoke his mind. "Maybe she wasn't happy with the conversation last night and decided to return to Elysia so she wouldn't be a burden on us."

"That's preposterous," Edward roared. "Did you forget already? She told us that Elysia was destroyed."

"Then, what would you suggest was her reason for leaving?" Brian leaned back in his chair, frustrated with the direction of the conversation.

"I don't know," Edward shouted, startling Katie back to reality. He closed his eyes in an attempt to get his swirling emotions back under some semblance of control. Endless seconds ticked by before his eyelids slowly reopened. "The one thing I do know is that this new development only serves to muddle our priorities and make my decision of what to do next that much more difficult. We don't exactly have numbers on our side and we can't really afford to split our group and start going in separate directions to compensate."

"Just pick something, Edward," Katie whispered softly, leaning her head wearily on his shoulder. "Like you said, we can only focus on one thing at a time. Whichever course of action you decide we should take, we will do everything in our power to get the task taken care of quickly so we can move on to the next objective."

Brooding, Edward remained silent for a couple of minutes. With a heavy sigh, he finally responded, "After carefully weighing our options, it pains me to say that chasing down and eradicating the demons that attacked us yesterday should probably be our first order of business. With them out of the picture, returning to other tasks would be much safer."

"If that's the case, it should be myself and Katie who hunt them down," Brian suggested. "Before you go getting all hot under the collar, I only say this because you need more time to heal. It would be pointless to have you along in your condition, and as for Jack ... if we have to do any significant climbing it would severely limit our progress. No offense, my friend," he remarked, glancing down at the wolf by Edward's feet.

Knowing that Brian spoke the truth, Edward nodded his agreement to the terms. "I have a stipulation to add," he replied, glancing up to meet the shaman's gaze. "If you run into more trouble than the two of you can handle on your own, please disengage from the fight and come back here. If we have to wait until I've healed enough to make the journey with you, then so be it."

"Fair enough," Brian agreed, glancing toward Katie to see if she did as well. "Perhaps we can wait an hour or two before we leave, though." He grinned, nodding his head in the direction of the disheveled brown hair adorning Edward's shoulder as her light snores broke the silence.

It was a couple of hours before dawn when George's persistence finally paid off. He had been biding his time, peering occasionally from the cracked open doorway, waiting impatiently for Brian to fall asleep. It almost seemed like he never would, but when his chin sunk to his chest after several long hours George didn't hesitate to take advantage of the opportunity. Sneaking past the slumbering shaman was the easy part. Victoria's body was light enough that he didn't have to concern himself with causing a floorboard to creak as he crept by, but opening the door to the outside was another matter entirely. The rusted hinges groaned as he snuck out into the night and George whipped his head around to make sure he hadn't alerted Brian. A momentary hitch in his light snores was the only reaction he gave to the sound.

Releasing his hold on the door, George allowed it to swing shut on its own, hoping the swift movement would lessen the amount of noise it would make as it closed. Swiftly, he darted around the side of the building where he stayed for a few moments, letting his breath out as noiselessly as he could. Once George was certain his exit from the inn had gone undetected, he slipped through the shadows to the next structure. As he walked along the front side of the dilapidated framework, searching for a way inside, he found a large, wooden panel, secured to a metal track about ten feet over his head. It reminded him of an old barn door. Gripping the edge he slid it aside, but only enough to squeeze through the opening.

The stable smelled of musty straw and decayed flesh, likely from prior rodent inhabitants which had starved to death when their food sources dried up. Though, there were still a number of corpses piled up behind the buildings so the stench might have just been seeping through the walls. With at least another hour or so before the first rays of sunshine would crest the horizon, George decided to look around. Keeping both hands ahead of him, sweeping back and forth through the darkness, he searched for anything that might be of use. After several minutes, and stumbling over a multitude of what were likely petrified horse turds, his eyes lit up. Underneath the palm of Victoria's hand was what felt like a coiled section of rope. *Perfect!*

Wasting no time, he gathered it up and searched for one of the ends. Once he found it, George sat the old woman's body against the wall of the stall and began to tightly bind Victoria's legs together. Her lips were twisted into a malicious grin by the evil entity inside of her. Fear quickly escalated in her mind as she read the thoughts of the invading spirit. Victoria's hands betrayed her will as they picked up the loose end of the rope, circling its coarse threads around her neck a few times before feeding it through a gap in the boards behind her. Pulling it tight, he knotted it around the bindings on her legs, crushing her windpipe and cutting off the air to her lungs as George leaned forward to secure the rope. He leaned back and forced a wicked smile to appear on her face when he finished. "You'll be perfectly fine as long as you hold still and don't try to escape," George's voice taunted within her mind.

Now that he no longer had to worry about losing his focus and accidentally allowing Victoria to come to the forefront, and very likely warning her son and his companions, he concentrated on exiting the fragile shell of the old woman. The added exertion he had caused her body by forcing it to move around beyond its normal limits, coupled with the emotional turmoil George had put her through, caused Victoria to pass out as he slipped from her body.

Cowering behind the willow tree at the edge of town, Amber watched things unfold, not daring to make her presence known until she knew for sure what was going on. She suspected that somehow the man who'd killed her, and seemed to be a ghost himself now, was inside of Edward's mother and controlling her like a puppet. She didn't have any proof of her suspicions to show her friends yet, but Amber was sure if she kept a close eye on things that the evidence would present itself soon.

Seemingly endless hours passed since she had seen everyone go inside of the inn, but just when she began to consider moving in for a closer look, Amber saw the old woman quietly sneak from the building and disappear inside the structure on the other side. After a short time she pondered moving in for a better view, her curiosity slowly beginning to overpower her fear. Before she could act on this impulse, however, Amber witnessed the one thing she dreaded most ... the ghost of her killer, peering from the partially open door of the stable!

Chapter 4

Remaining hidden in the secret cellar of the farmhouse, the Black Knight sensed that his plans would soon be set in motion. If, that was, the younger version of George complied with his will. He was hopeful. The man *did* seem significantly easier to manipulate and control than his willful, older counterpart back on Desolace, but the jury was still out on whether this was going to be a waste of his time, or the most brilliant solution he had ever come up with.

"Will you shut up?" the Black Knight snapped at the screaming plaything George had left behind. Her nude body trembled in the chains which secured her to a sturdy ring in the concrete floor. The sound of his voice caused a stream of urine to gush down her leg, the warm liquid briefly pooling near her shackled feet before it trickled into the drain a foot or two in front of her. The shrill pitch of the woman's screams, muffled though they were by the gag in her mouth, penetrated his head like an axe splitting firewood. He contemplated silencing her for good, but reconsidered. *Maybe, once George has carried out his mission, I could have him drag her with us. No sense in destroying a perfectly acceptable subject that I can put to use when I get back to Cemetery Hill.*

Slipping through the heavy, steel door separating the torture chamber from the remainder of the house, the

Black Knight quietly ascended the stone staircase which terminated at the bookcase. Placing an ear to the back side of it, he listened for movement. The muffled sound of voices filtered through the wood. A wicked smile creased his face. *Oh, he is good*, the Black Knight thought. *It is no wonder that he captures his victims so easily. The man has the silver tongue of a demon.* Restraining a chuckle, he continued to eavesdrop until the voices receded.

Waiting a few moments longer to make sure he could pass to the opposite side of the shelf undetected, he slid the panel aside quietly and stepped through into the living room. Stealthily moving into the hallway, the Black Knight cocked his head slightly to one side. The whispered sounds of voices were just barely perceptible, but they seemed to indicate that the humans were preparing to turn in for the night.

His curiosity getting the better of him, he crept silently up the staircase. It wasn't as if the Black Knight had never witnessed death, more mortals had suffered that fate by his own hands than he could even begin to count, but he wanted more than anything to see George in action. That was just how his brain was wired. He had a compulsive need to bask himself in the misery and death of others.

Several darkened doorways greeted him as he turned into the upper hallway at the top of the stairs. Moonlight filtered through a lone window at the opposite end of the corridor. Twisted shadows danced eerily on the walls, courtesy of the swaying branches of the large oak in the front yard. In this fractured light, the Black Knight could see that all but one of the doors lining the hallway were closed. One, at the very end of the hall, had a hint of luminescence shining beneath it. Another, from the room directly beside the first, was cracked open.

Ignoring the portals closest to him, the stained wood of their panels firmly shut with no sound or light emanating from them, the Black Knight glided down the hall like a child attempting to sneak up on Santa Claus in the middle of the night, hoping to catch the jolly fellow leaving presents under the Christmas tree. Hearing the whimpering, stifled cries of a child resonating in the darkened corridor, as if the tiny human had its face buried in a pillow, he stopped next to the partially opened door. Impatiently, he waited for the child to quiet down, hoping that when she did it would signal it was safe for him to pass by so he could listen in on George and his wife. More than anything, the Black Knight desired to hear what deceptive words young George would use to lull the woman into a false sense of security. He was also eager to watch the man fulfill his demand and prove his loyalty to him.

Upset because she had to go to bed without getting to pillage the king's ransom of candy she had hauled in tonight, Cassie pulled her covers up to her chin. Grabbing the pillow from beneath her head, she buried her face in its feathery depths. She didn't want her parents to hear her wailing sobs because they would likely think she was being a spoiled brat, which would only cause them to withhold her candy even longer. Well … that wasn't the only reason she was crying. The creepy shadows in the hall outside of her room were scaring Cassie, too, even though her daddy had explained what caused them. Knowing they were the branches of the tree in the front yard did nothing to calm her fears when she could see the shadows scratching at the walls like the long, skeletal fingers of a hideous monster.

Fighting to choke back her sobs, Cassie sniffled and took a deep breath. Lifting the pillow off her blonde curls and pushing it toward the headboard of her bed, she listened to see if her parents had heard the commotion of her wails. Their voices hadn't change, remaining soft enough as they penetrated the wall between the two rooms that Cassie couldn't make out what they were saying. To her, it almost sounded the same as Charlie Brown's teacher in the Peanuts cartoons.

Catching a flicker of movement in the hallway from the corner of her puffy, tear-reddened eyes, Cassie turned her head expecting to see her daddy. Instead, she was greeted by the glowing, elongated face of a clown. Closing her eyes in hopes that it was something her frightened imagination had conjured up, she counted to three in her head before opening them. The face was still staring into the room, its shimmering yellow eyes boring into her. Unable to look away from the horrible sight, Cassie screamed at the top of her lungs.

Talking softly as she lay beside George in their bed, Jen relayed the events of her trick-or-treat outing with Cassie. Listening to her tale with all the attentiveness of a good husband, he nodded and smiled in all the right places, even though his mind worked furiously as he contemplated the Black Knight's demands. He had to be the perfect actor if he had any intention of carrying out the demon's request without raising his wife's suspicions. After relaying her story, she turned off the light on her nightstand then scooted in closer to snuggle with George. Draping her arm over him, she pulled her husband to her lips and kissed him goodnight.

Jen was on the verge of falling asleep a few minutes later when an ear shattering scream broke the silence, causing her to sit up in bed so quickly that you would have thought she had been jabbed with a cattle prod. First she spun her head toward the closed bedroom door, then whipped it back toward George to see if he was awake. A small amount of light filtered through the blinds drawn down over the window, but it was just enough for Jen to see her husband sitting up on the other side of the bed.

"I'll go check on Cassie." He sighed, feeling the urgent, panicked jostling of his wife. "She probably just had a nightmare," he added, hoping to calm Jen. Rising from the mattress, George stumbled through the darkness to the door and felt around for the knob. Swinging it open fully so his wife could hear what was going on better, he stepped into the hall and turned toward his daughter's room.

As he approached her door, George noticed something lying on the floor. Bending down to pick up the object, he suddenly became very angry. "Where are you, you bastard?" Squinting into the shadows, his eyes flicked from one area to the next, trying to find the entity which contacted him earlier and was likely nearby. The deformed clown mask he held in his hand was evidence that the demon hadn't stayed put in the basement.

Turning toward his daughter's bedroom after a fruitless visual search for the creature, he couldn't help but wonder. Was the foul monster growing impatient because he hadn't carried out his orders immediately? Was it taking matters into its own hands and killing his family while he slept, perhaps thinking he was a coward that wouldn't do it? Whatever the reasoning was behind the mask's appearance in the hallway, there was only one way to find out.

Reaching through the narrow opening that the cracked door provided, his fingers fumbled across the wall for the light switch. Flicking it up, the room was bathed in the pinkish illumination of the decorative cover of the light fixture on the ceiling. Before him, Cassie cowered against the headboard of her bed, her tiny face buried in the pillow she clutched to her chest, allowing only a fraction of her blonde curls to be seen.

Relaxing slightly when he saw his daughter alive, George sauntered over and sat down on the mattress beside her, placing a gentle hand on the back of her head. "Did you have a nightmare, honey?" Though his soft tone of voice would normally soothe her enough to warrant a hug, this time she didn't even look up at him. Instead, she shook her head vehemently in the feathery depths of her pillow.

"There was a monster standing in the hall, looking at me, Daddy," she cried. "I think it wanted to eat me."

"Well, it's not there anymore, honey. I must have scared it away when I came to check on you," he whispered, dropping the mask on the bed beside him and pulling the pillow from Cassie's grip so he could see her face. George pulled his daughter toward him and hugged her tightly to his chest.

She sniffled for a few moments before turning her head upward to look at him. "Can I sleep with you and Mommy tonight? I promise I'll be good," she pleaded.

"Of course, sweetheart," he replied, playfully ruffling her hair. Cassie wrapped her arms and legs around him happily, a smile creasing her tear-stained face for the first time since George had sat down beside her. Pushing himself up from the mattress, his daughter clung to him like a leech. Temporarily forgetting about the clown mask, which still rested on Cassie's bed, he turned the light off, exited the room, and walked back to his own bed chamber.

Jen met them in the doorway, the look of a terrified mother etched across her features. "Is she okay?" Before George could answer, she ran her hands lightly over her daughter as if she were searching for a mortal wound.

Reaching out, George put a finger beneath her chin and tilted her head up to meet his eyes. "She's fine, baby. She thought she saw a monster and asked if she could sleep with us tonight."

A thin, tight-lipped smile appeared on Jen's face and she sighed through her nose in relief. Her bright blue eyes shimmered with unshed tears of happiness. "Of course you can, angel," she remarked, leaning forward and kissing the back of Cassie's head.

The excitement of the night's events had passed. Jen and Cassie were cuddled close to each other and sleeping soundly. Normally, Jen's light snores would be like a lullaby to him, but it wasn't the case tonight. His mind was restless and sleep eluded him as George lay in the darkness, staring at the ceiling and contemplating what he should do the next time he crossed paths with the demon that demanded he kill his family.

Chapter 5

Katie stirred from her slumber as the first rays of dawn began to filter through the doorway of the inn. Wincing at the stiffness in her neck, she rubbed the tightened muscles absently. "What?" She glanced sternly into the grinning face of the red-haired shaman across the table from her.

"Nothing," he laughed, spotting the small puddle of her drool on Edward's shoulder.

"Once you are more fully awake, you and Brian should get going," Edward remarked, turning his gaze to meet Katie's sleep reddened and puffy brown eyes.

A cloud of confusion crossed her features temporarily, but it quickly cleared when her foggy memory began to recall their earlier conversation. Rubbing her hands briskly over her face and lightly slapping her cheeks to speed up the process of waking, Brian once again burst into a fit of laughter.

"What's so freaking funny?" Katie glared at him, despising being the brunt of a joke.

Quickly he regained his composure, though it was hard to see because he hung his head. "I'm sorry, Katie," he apologized. "Guess it's just been a long night and things that I wouldn't normally find amusing I am finding more hilarious than they probably are."

She sat in silence for a couple of minutes before she

realized that she was being a bitch again, likely snapping at him because she'd barely slept at all in the last day or so. Raising her head, she met Brian's expectant blue eyes, the look in them telling her that he was waiting to see if she would accept his apology. "I'm sorry, too, Brian. I didn't mean to sound so harsh."

"No big deal." He smiled weakly. "I should have known better than to pick on you right after you woke up. I probably would have been grumpy, too, if the shoe had been on the other foot."

Attempting to return his smile to let him know there weren't any hard feelings, Katie's mouth opened in a cavernous yawn, interrupting the grin and twisting it into something that made her look deformed. Brian bit his cheek to suppress the urge to chuckle. "Perhaps we should gather our things and get going," he suggested, trying his best to divert his attention in order to restrain another outburst.

Nodding in agreement, Katie turned to face Edward. "What about you? I'm still not entirely comfortable leaving you here alone, especially in your condition."

"I won't be alone," he replied, grimacing as he reached down to stroke the fur of the wolf by his feet. "I have Jack to keep me company." Still, even so, he longed to be able to make the journey with his friends and couldn't help but worry about their safety. "Don't forget to pack a saddlebag to take with you. There's no telling how long it will be before you return," he added.

"We'll be fine," Katie consoled, lightly patting Edward's shoulder. "If we run into trouble, Brian can fast fry the opposition like we're having our own private barbecue."

"Either that, or I could turn the enemy inside out," Brian joked, "but that's only if Katie doesn't kick the crap out of them first."

"PMS is a bitch." She laughed with a wink toward the red-haired shaman.

"Ha, ha," Brian smirked as he pushed his chair out from the table and rose to his feet. "I'll be outside if you need me for anything before we go," he told Edward, "packing a bag and making sure we don't forget anything."

It wasn't long before Brian and Katie poked their heads back through the front door of the inn to check on Edward one last time. His arms, tucked beneath his long, black hair, rested on the table before him. He raised his weary dome to focus his pale eyes on their shadowy figures.

"We're preparing to leave now," Brian announced. "Are you sure you don't need anything before we go?"

Edward shook his head in response. "Getting some rest and allowing my wounds time to heal are my primary concerns. As long as you left at least *some* of the supplies behind for me, I should be fine until you both return."

"We will try to make this journey as swift as we can, but since we have no idea what we may be up against, I can't make any promises. For all I know, it could only take a day or less, but I'm not going to hold my breath or try to give you false hope."

"With the way my luck has been running lately …"

Edward trailed off, not wanting to voice his concerns of the possibility that he might never see them again.

Katie peered over Brian's shoulder at their haggard leader, waiting for him to finish his sentence. When Edward remained silent, she understood the implications of why he hadn't completed the thought. Her shoulders slumped as she sunk down and turned her head so the men wouldn't see the well of tears threatening to leak from her eyes. When she had regained her composure, Katie tugged on Brian's sleeve and motioned with her head that they should go. Before he could add to the sadness of the moment, the red-haired shaman offered a nod and a wave to Edward, then turned to follow Katie.

"Good luck, my friends," Edward mumbled to their backs as they walked away. He only hoped that it wouldn't be the last time he saw them.

The two of them shuffled around to the back side of the inn. Both were too choked up with the departure to speak, until they left the shelter of the buildings behind and approached the railroad tracks masked by the overgrowth of weeds at the edge of town. Bending down next to the rusted rails, Katie glanced to her left and saw that the tracks seemed to terminate about one hundred feet away. Turning her head in the opposite direction, she saw a bend in the rails, which appeared to head directly into the forest, and toward the mountainous hill beyond. "Looks like we're going that way," she told Brian, pointing to her right.

With the light of day upon him, George could no longer see the ghostly nuisance which seemed to follow his every move. For a brief moment, he was grateful for the reprieve, but at the same time disappointed when he concluded that he wouldn't be able to torture the woman by making her watch what he did to people. A flicker of comprehension dawned on him, causing a twisted grin to cross his face when he realized that *his* form was similarly invisible. *I could have some real fun with this! Even though I can no longer touch, and savor, my victims, being a ghost could prove to be just as amusing! Maybe even more so!* His mind swirled with possibilities as he watched two of his adversaries exit the inn.

Allowing his transparent form to drift effortlessly, he followed in their wake to spy on them, wondering why they had left their injured friends behind in the inn. Seeing the girl bend down a short distance from the rear of the building, intently studying the railroad tracks, George began to think that his luck would continue. When he saw her point to the section of rails heading away from town and up the mountain, this feeling became an almost certainty. Even so, he patiently waited until he saw them start to follow the tracks, disappearing from sight in the dense underbrush beside the rails.

Rubbing his invisible hands together with maniacal glee, George floated toward the entrance of the inn. *Time to turn up the heat and make things interesting!* When he got to the front of the structure he became agitated. The door was shut! Frustrated with the delay of his playtime, he began searching for another way into the building.

Slowly circling the inn, George drifted from one window to the next, each one yielding the same results. His anger was on the verge of boiling over when he spotted his salvation. High above him, a small, attic window was propped open with a stick, presumably to keep the uppermost floor of the structure from getting too warm. This time of year it should have been closed up tight like the rest of the windows, but apparently someone had neglected their duty. Perhaps the individual who should have taken care of this assignment was lying with the rest of the corpses piled against the rear of the building.

Quickly taking advantage of the open portal, George entered the attic. After a brief search, he located a stairway leading down to the lower levels. In his excitement, he zipped down the steps, only to come to another closed door blocking his path. At this point, George was grateful he was no longer alive. If he were, he would almost certainly have developed an instant migraine from the overwhelming rage he now felt. His anger was so strong that it was clouding his thoughts. Attempting to close his eyes so he could take a deep breath and relax only heightened his already volatile emotions, realizing that in his current state he could not close his eyelids to block everything from sight because they were transparent.

Returning to the attic, George flitted furiously from one end to the other, desperately trying to figure out how to get at the injured people somewhere below him. Pacing back and forth managed to dissipate his murderous rage, but only slightly. With his anger retarded a notch, the solution suddenly became clear. *The old woman is the key! If I infest her crinkled shell again I will be able to interact with the physical world once more. It might actually be more satisfying to see the look in her son's eyes when he believes his own flesh and blood is taking his life.*

Drifting back outside through the propped open window, George sped toward the stable to retrieve the old woman's body. As he rounded the corner of the building, a noise emanating from somewhere to his right drew his attention. Searching for the source of the sound, his eyes settled on the haggard-looking wizard, rifling through the contents of a saddlebag. George watched the man take something from the pack, shoving the item in his mouth before untying the straps which held the worn, burlap sack in place on the back of the mechanical horse.

Out of the corner of his eye, George caught a glimpse of the opportunity he'd been looking for. The front door of the inn was partially open! Wasting no time, he quickly floated inside. Immediately upon his entry, a snarling, three-legged wolf greeted him with bared fangs.

Chapter 6

Though the underbrush they traveled through was dense, the railroad tracks they were following blazed a trail through the tangled foliage quite effectively, allowing Katie and Brian to make good time thus far. After an hour, two at the most, they found themselves at the foot of a rickety bridge. Even though some of the boards which supported the tracks were decayed, some to the extent that they had fallen to the river rushing below it, there didn't seem to be any damage to the rails themselves. Obviously, if the dilapidated bridge had been sturdy enough to withstand the weight of a rail-car, the two of them should have no trouble making the crossing without incident.

After a brief discussion, Brian and Katie decided to take a quick, five minute break. Even though the morning air was cool, and they were both in decent physical shape because of all the walking they did every day, Brian was on the verge of a full-blown sweat. Wiping the perspiration from her brow, Katie plopped down on the edge of the bridge, allowing her legs to dangle over the side. Peeling his sweat dampened tunic over his head, Brian sat down beside her, fanning his shirt out on the wood next to him in hopes the sun would dry it a bit.

"Oh my God, Brian! Put that thing back on! You could blind someone with that pasty whiteness," Katie teased, dramatically shielding her eyes.

"Ha, ha," he smirked. "I've never been a big fan of exposing my skin to the sun, but I think all redheads feel the same way."

"I was only picking," she explained with a grin. "Though I don't share your condition, I'm well aware of the fact that people with red hair sunburn very easily. I was just trying to keep the mood light. The task before us will likely take that away from us soon enough. Might as well smile and be happy while we still can."

Knowing she spoke the truth, he rubbed his chin thoughtfully. Glancing toward what lay ahead for them, Brian traced the path of the rails with his eyes. It was impossible to tell from where he sat, but if he wasn't mistaken their journey would be more treacherous from here on out. The tangled brush swallowed the tracks shortly after emerging on the opposite side of the river, but he could see dots of shiny reflections at irregular intervals upon the fairly steep incline of the hill, which by his estimation would take them an hour or less to reach.

Brian's silence was beginning to make Katie nervous. *Is he angry with me for making fun of him? Or, does he know something that he's not telling me?* "Are you all right?"

"Sorry, I was lost in thought," he replied, shaking his head as he turned to face her, noticing a hint of panic in her voice. "I didn't mean to worry you."

She offered him a thin smile, believing he was hiding something from her. "Ready to get moving again?"

"I suppose we should. The sooner we get this business taken care of, the better." He sighed, picking up his shirt and pulling it on.

Standing up, they gathered their things and began to cross the bridge. It was a more tedious journey than what they had endured to this point. Footing was perilous at best. The missing planks were easy enough to avoid, but the wood of some of the other boards was more rotten than they would have thought them to be. Especially considering that the rails showed no indication of flaws in the supporting structure. When they had managed to get within fifty feet of the end of the bridge, Brian began to relax slightly. Just as he did, a loud *crack* broke the silence. Spinning around toward the sound, he reacted just quick enough to keep Katie from plunging to the rushing water below by grabbing hold of her wrist as her leg plummeted through a rotten plank.

"Son of a bitch!" Katie grimaced in agony as the pressure of Brian's grip caused a sudden flare of pain in her broken hand. Grasping his forearm with her good hand, she eased the tension on her screaming appendage just enough to keep from passing out as Brian hauled her up from the ragged hole. Once Katie was on solid ground again, she gingerly inspected her fractured extremity.

"I'm sorry. It all happened so fast. I didn't have time to consider which of your hands was injured before I latched on," he apologized, wincing as he watched her prod and massage the damaged appendage, checking to see if the incident had made matters worse.

"It's okay. I prefer a healthy dose of pain as opposed to death," she confessed.

"You've got a point," he remarked with a half smile. Shifting his position so she could throw her good arm over his shoulder, he wrapped an arm around her waist. "Let's get you off this bridge before something else happens."

Using Brian as a crutch, she hobbled her way to dry land before easing herself to the ground. Katie tenderly checked her leg as he anxiously watched. The broken plank she had fallen through had ripped a foot-long gash in her leather pants. Widening the gap so she could inspect the flesh beneath, she saw an angry red stripe on her skin where the board had bit into her. The section of her leg that had come into contact with the jagged plank first, the area just above her kneecap, was the only part of the scrape which was bleeding. "Minor flesh wound," she announced, meeting Brian's worried gaze. "Can you grab me a strip of cloth from the pack?"

He quickly complied, rummaging in the pack and pulling out one of the few remnants of cloth inside which had made the journey from future Earth when they'd been fighting for their very lives against the hordes of undead. "Thanks." She smiled, snatching the strip of cloth from his hand. Tucking it through the tear in her pants, she encircled the wound on her thigh just tight enough to put pressure on it to stanch the flow of blood, then pulled the ends out of the hole. Pinching the leather together, Katie wound the remaining material around the outside of her pants and knotted it firmly. Holding out her good hand, she gestured for Brian to help her up. Once she was on her feet again, she attempted to hide the grimace of pain as she shifted her weight to the injured leg.

"Should we go back to the inn, or do you think you can go on?"

Katie hesitated a moment before answering, subconsciously asking herself the same question. "I should be okay," she finally said, unsure if her words were a lie to comfort him. The one thing she *did* know was that she didn't want to return to the inn and tell Edward they had failed to reach their objective. "I'm sure that once we get moving again, it will start feeling better," she added, seeing the skeptical look on his face.

"I hope you're right," he stated with a tight-lipped, half smile.

Thankfully, after the first half an hour of resuming their trek, Katie's wounded leg was bothering her less and less. Her broken hand, however, was another matter entirely. Ever since Brian had grabbed her wrist to save her life, and put the pressure of her suspended body weight on it, the extremity had been throbbing like an infected tooth. It hadn't been a huge issue, but that seemed about to change. Just ahead, the railroad tracks were beginning to wind steadily upward, which meant she would be required to do some climbing very soon. Hopefully, it wouldn't be a steep enough incline that she would need to worry. Especially when she considered that a rail-car had traveled these tracks without getting derailed, though, that said nothing of her needing to use the broken hand to maintain her balance. If push came to shove she would rather grasp something with it and endure the agony than tumble back down the hill, which could potentially be far more devastating to her wellbeing.

Brian stopped for a minute and glanced behind him. "Having second thoughts?"

"Just catching my breath," she wheezed.

Nodding, he put his hands on his hips and turned away from her to study the tracks. Their path was slightly easier to see, now that they had emerged from the thickest of the foliage which had shrouded them from sight earlier. Craning his head upward, he still could not make out where they were going. For all he knew these rails could go on for miles, cresting the hill they were climbing and running down the other side like a medieval rollercoaster.

"Okay, I'm ready to go again," Katie announced, startling Brian from his thoughts.

"Are you sure you don't need help?" He scrutinized her expression as he awaited her response.

"Nope, I'm good," she replied, giving him a thumbs up.

With an almost imperceptible nod, he turned and resumed the long, uphill trudge.

Chapter 7

It was obvious upon his entering the inn that the wolf before him could at the very least sense his presence, possibly even see him. Forced into making a quick decision, George weighed his options while he still had time. He would be trapped if the wizard came back inside and shut the door. Attempting to infiltrate and possess the animal in front of him didn't seem like a viable solution, though he couldn't be absolutely sure. The logistics of trying such a thing seemed doomed to failure. The physics of transferring his ghostly essence into a creature which did not share the same physical attributes as humans was a conundrum George had never tested, making it impossible for him to know if it could be done. There was always the possibility that his arms could slide into the animal's forelegs, but the more he thought about it, the less sure he was about the potential outcome.

Deciding to test a theory, he allowed himself to drift backwards and to the left, hoping to determine if the animal could indeed see him, or track his movements. Indicating that it could, the wolf rose from the floor, turning its head in his direction with its eyes focused intently on him.

Edward appeared in the doorway, poking his head inside. "What's all the fuss about, Jack?" The wolf seemed to ignore his question, his gleaming eyes remaining locked on some unseen threat he perceived. As his mind furiously reeled with possibilities, an idea struck him. *It could be a ghost, like Amber! We've only been able to see her when the sun was down, even though she's told us before that she is usually nearby. Although, I seriously doubt Jack would act this way if it were indeed her.* The gears in his head turned, rapidly searching for the answer which seemed just beyond his grasp. Suddenly it hit him. Even though he had never encountered a ghost other than Amber, it was entirely possible that an unfamiliar entity had found its way to them, perhaps brought here by Amber herself!

Testing his hypothesis, he took a step backward and swung the door shut. With the ambient light source cut off the interior of the inn grew dim, the grime-coated windows allowing only a hint of the morning sun to penetrate their panes. Edward closed his eyes for a moment, hoping it would force them to adjust to the dimness a few seconds faster. When he opened them, he squinted toward the area that Jack seemed to be focused upon. Were his eyes playing tricks on him? If not, there was a hazy, man-shaped mist hanging in the air before him, looking much like someone's reflection in a dirty mirror.

The sound of the closing door startled George. Daring to take his eyes off of the wolf before him, he whipped his head toward the man. It took a few seconds for him to figure out why the wizard had done what he did, but as the man reopened his eyes and looked in his direction, squinting for a moment before a shocked look of recognition appeared on his pasty face, George suddenly knew the game was up. The wizard was staring directly at him!

On the verge of panic, seeing his plans swirling down the drain, he knew he had to make a decision … now! His first instinct was to flee and hide, giving him more time to come up with a concrete plan of action, but with the way the wolf was locked onto him now, it didn't seem like a very good option. *Chances are, that beast would be on my trail the whole time.* As if to punctuate this point, Jack inched closer, baring his massive fangs and snarling viciously. George had nearly resigned himself to taking his chances and trying to hide when the solution to his dilemma smacked him like a tire iron to the skull.

Hoping to catch Edward off guard, George rushed toward him. Maybe it was the wizard's weakened state, but whatever the reason, the penetration of his fleshy exterior went easier than he could have anticipated. Within moments, he had plunged into the man's core, immediately stretching his form to match that of his host, like putting on a twisted Halloween skin-suit. He didn't come forward and take control of the man's body right away, but instead watched and waited, looking to see how the wolf would react.

In his injured state, Edward was unable to dodge the oncoming misty form of his adversary. He let out a shocked gasp as the ghost passed through his skin, expecting the sensation to be more painful than it actually was. Once the initial surprise wore off, he gazed around, disoriented and frightened, almost as if he was anticipating another of the Black Knight's creepy minions to suddenly jump out of the shadows to attack him. When nothing of the sort happened, he turned back to regard Jack, who stared at him with the same look of bafflement he felt. "Where did it go, Jack?" Taking a tentative step toward the wolf, he crouched down and stroked his fur, attempting to calm the confused beast and himself at the same time.

The instant Edward laid a hand on him, Jack began to whimper and nervously shuffled back a few steps. "What's wrong, Jack?" Unable to comprehend his friend's reaction to his touch, he sat down on the dusty floor and patted the wooden planks beside him. The wolf did not approach him immediately, but instead cocked its head in nervous curiosity, as if it was having the same trouble grasping the concept of what had just transpired as Edward was. Then, before his very eyes, Jack's demeanor seemed to change after raising his snout and taking a whiff of the stale air in the room.

"What is it, Jack?" Edward's voice crackled with nervousness as the animal began stalking toward him as if it no longer recognized him. When the beast was within a couple of feet of him, its upper lip pulled upward, saliva dripping from its exposed fangs. Refusing to use his magic to restrain his friend, Edward continued talking in a soothing tone of voice. When Jack's teeth gnashed together inches from his face as the wolf lunged forward, he knew that keeping his magic bottled up inside of him was no longer an option.

As he began to summon a spell to repel the crazed animal, Edward's eyes lost their focus as George shoved his way forward to take control of his body. Maybe it was the difference which glinted in the steely, gray orbs in the eye sockets of Edward's skull that tipped the wolf off to his presence, but it no longer mattered. With control over the wizard's body, he wasn't just an impotent and intangible being; he could now pull the man's strings like an expert puppeteer.

Lowering his center of gravity, Jack prepared to attack, coiling his good leg beneath him like a serpent that was about to strike. Saliva dripped from his jowls as he opened his mouth wide and launched himself through the air at Edward.

A split second before the wolf's jaws would have snapped shut on his face, Edward's hands shot up from his sides and grasped the animal around the neck with a strength that was not his own. Squeezing with all of his might, George dug the wizard's fingernails into Jack's flesh, puncturing the wolf's hide and causing blood to spurt from the wounds. Pushing his front paws against Edward's chest, Jack struggled to break free of his grip. Choking, blood began to gurgle in his throat and his makeshift hindquarter scratched weakly at Edward's clothing. After a few moments, his legs hung limply from his torso and his head lolled to one side at an unnatural angle.

Edward regained consciousness a short time later, feeling as if he were rising from the depths of a nightmare. His head throbbed with an ache unlike any he had ever dealt with before, but it wasn't the only part of him that hurt. Pushing himself up from the floor, where he'd apparently collapsed, he grimaced in agony as his muscles protested. Managing to at least get to an upright, sitting position, he was greeted by the sight of carnage he wasn't prepared to see. Body parts appeared to be flung carelessly in every direction, human body parts. A severed arm lying by his foot, a twisted rope of intestines a few inches from that, and a little further to his right was what looked to be a partial leg. Fearing the worst had happened, Edward raised his hands, intending to cup them around his mouth to yell for his friend, even though the evidence before him suggested that he'd been killed. As his hands passed in front of his face, he saw they were slick with sticky, half-dried blood. Just then, an awful realization struck him with explosive force. He wasn't sure how it had happened, but Edward knew that his own hands had been Jack's undoing. Turning his head away from the carnage, he vomited violently. Wiping his mouth with his sleeve, he saw the one thing he had hoped to never see … Jack's decapitated head lying on the floor in the corner of the room, staring back at him accusingly. "Oh my God! What have I done?"

Chapter 8

Judging by the position of the fiery orb in the sky it was early afternoon. Their uphill progress, slow as it might have seemed, was relatively quick when they considered the angle of their ascent, which at times was borderline vertical. How the rail-car had traversed the length of the track, and made it to the bottom of the hill without flying off of the rails, was a topic that defied logic. Then there was the matter of its return trip, ignoring the laws of physics and gravity as the rail-car had made the seemingly impossible climb.

As if to punctuate just how arduous their journey had been to this point, Katie stopped to catch her breath, wiping the sweat from her brow with the back of her broken hand. Leaning forward to balance her center of gravity, she took a quick look over her shoulder to see how far they had come. The dizzying height caused her to gulp loudly. Though the foliage below her nearly obscured the abandoned town at the base of the hill, she could just barely make out the dilapidated buildings, looking like nothing more than mere specks from her vantage point. Quickly, she turned back to face the tracks before the woozy feeling weakened her knees and caused her to plummet to the bottom of the hill, knowing if she were to fall from this high up that there would be nothing more than bits and pieces of her body left.

Brian also paused his ascent when he realized he could no longer hear Katie's labored breathing. Digging his fingers into the dirt above a railroad tie, he grasped the beam as tightly as he could manage, and tilted his head to the left to glance behind him. When he gazed down at Katie's uplifted face, her tight-lipped expression and raised eyebrows put him on the edge of panic. "What's wrong?" He tried to remain calm, but the nervousness in his voice betrayed him.

"I'm scared," she admitted, "and I'm beginning to wonder if this is a good idea."

"Why would you think that? Is your hand bothering you? Are you afraid of falling?" His questions flew with such rapidity that he didn't even pause to take a breath between them.

"Well, I wasn't really freaked out about falling until I looked down." She laughed nervously. "As for my hand, I think I can block out the pain enough to continue on. What scares me more than anything, though, is the thought of leaving Edward behind in his condition. I'm worried about something happening down there and us being too far away to help."

Having had the same exact thoughts before they had embarked on their uphill journey, Brian frowned. After a few moments of silence, the worry lines which creased his forehead gradually dissolved. "There's no point in fretting about the things we can't change." He sighed. "For now, we need to concentrate on carrying out his wishes. The sooner we can get this dilemma taken care of, the sooner we can get back. Hopefully, by the time we return, Edward will be healed enough to resume traveling."

"True," Katie admitted, letting out a breath she hadn't realized she had been holding. "I only hope this doesn't turn out to be a pointless errand. I mean, for all we know, those creatures could be long gone by now."

Even though he had no desire to burst her bubble, his lips pressed together in a grim line. "I don't think that's an issue." He frowned, earning himself a questioning look from her. Before she could open her mouth to ask what he meant, Brian continued. "I've been sensing something for the last ten minutes or so, but so far it hasn't been strong enough to be considered an immediate threat."

Katie gasped, her expression a mixture of confusion and unease. "Why didn't you say something before now?"

"I didn't think it was a big deal," he remarked, averting her demanding stare.

"How can you possibly think it's not a big deal?"

"I'm sorry ... I didn't want to needlessly worry you. I swear I would've said something before now if the feeling had been stronger," he apologized.

"Please, don't keep me out of the loop. Getting caught off guard is something neither of us can afford to do," Katie stated, her tone softening slightly.

Feeling chastised, he was about to tell her he wouldn't hold anything back from her in the future when a noise from above them distracted him. Whipping his head around toward the sound, he saw a cascade of small, pebble-sized rocks coming right at them, bounding down the hill as if someone had lost their footing above them for a second. "Cover your eyes," he yelled, raising a hand to shield his own from the falling debris.

As the tiny avalanche of stones bounced past them,

the sound of cackling laughter erupted above them. Turning her face upward, Katie caught a brief glimpse of movement. "I think we've walked into a trap," she declared, attempting to maintain her balance as she craned her neck, trying to get a better look. "I'm not positive, but I think the demons that attacked Edward are hiding behind that outcropping." She pointed toward it, holding the pose just long enough for Brian to follow the angle of her finger.

Quickly glancing from left to right, looking for shelter from the rock-slide, he shouted back to Katie, "I think we need to take cover in the trees. Maybe we can work our way close enough for them to be in range of—"

"I don't think that's an option, Brian," she interrupted, nervously casting a look to either side of the rails. "I'll never make it without sliding to the bottom of the hill. Remember? I only have one good hand!"

I need an alternative ... before those demons decide to throw something larger than a pebble down at us! He pounded the palm of one hand against his forehead as if it would somehow, miraculously forcibly eject a usable idea from his brain. Scrambling to come up with a plan that would work, he mentally flipped through every possible scenario he could think of. Suddenly, his eyes glimmered with hope. "Climb up to where I am. I have an idea."

As Katie ventured upward in compliance, she saw Brian shifting away from the tracks toward a pine tree which poked out of the rocky ground a few feet from the rails. "What are you doing? I'll never make it over there without slipping," she grunted with effort as she climbed to where he'd been standing a moment ago.

"Just keep going," he urged. "Trust me. I have a plan."

Glancing uneasily toward him as she attained Brian's prior position, she saw him extending his arm out to her, coaxing her to grab hold of his hand. She looked at the precarious slant of his body, one hand wrapped around the slender trunk of the tree in front of him, his booted feet braced on a large rock embedded in the earth. The sound of more debris falling from above prodded Katie into motion. Reaching out with her good hand, she fought the urge to close her eyes. Feeling his fingers lock tightly around her wrist, she held her breath as he tugged her toward him. Her feet flailed beneath her for a moment, making her look like she was running on an inclined treadmill, before sliding into his ankle and grinding to a halt.

"Son of a …" He winced at the sudden pressure on his joint, the pain forcing him to wonder if she had dislocated it.

"Don't let go," Katie pleaded, wrapping her arms around him so tightly that Brian felt like a large boa constrictor was attempting to squeeze the life from him.

"Grab on to the tree," he wheezed, trying to pry her vise-like grip from his torso. "I can't breathe."

At first she didn't hear what he had said, the utter panic of the situation clouding her mind. When she realized his words were not part of a vivid daydream, the fog began to dissipate and her clinging grip loosened enough for her to shift her position, allowing her to grasp the pine in the same manner as Brian had. "Sorry," she whispered sheepishly.

Verin had turned his attention from the assemblage of impish demons, which were clustered together just outside the mountain entrance to Cemetery Hill, furious that they had failed to dispatch the mortals in the town below. As he stormed through the nearly empty chamber, intending to return to the Black Knight's throne room to check and see if he could locate his master's whereabouts by studying the monitors, the tiny creatures began to cackle with delight. Whipping his head around to investigate the commotion, Verin saw them gathering handfuls of small rocks and chucking them downhill from the precipice where the platform rail-car rested.

Spinning toward the ruckus, he marched outside to admonish them for their behavior. "Knock it off," he scolded, his features twisting with rage. "You idiots are acting like children!"

The boldest of the lesser demons spun to face him. "In case you haven't noticed, there are two of the humans from below attempting to scale the mountain," he retorted angrily. "We are merely trying to keep them at bay, and with any luck cause them to fall. Why can't we have a little fun while we're doing our job?"

His forehead crinkled in thought as Verin slowly drifted to the edge of the outcropping and peered over the top of a sizable boulder at the terrain below. At first he didn't see anything noteworthy, but as he made to turn away he caught a glimpse of red hair peeking out from behind a tree trunk at the limit of his vision. Growling at the temerity of the humans, he whipped his head around and glared at the bolder minion. "Whatever you do, make sure the mortals don't reach Cemetery Hill," Verin spat. "Stop pelting them with those pebbles! Make them think the threat has passed so they will begin climbing again, and once they get too close to dodge it, heave the boulder down upon them and pulverize their bones to dust!"

Chapter 9

Standing in the open doorway of the inn, having used Edward's body to give himself a way out before relinquishing control of his fleshy shell, George watched the wizard draw the conclusion that he had killed his werewolf friend. The man's thin frame heaved, tears of anguish streaming down his dirty, blood smeared cheeks as his chin sunk to his chest, blubbering like a child who had lost his favorite toy. It seemed as if it had been forever since George had reveled in the glee of torture. He savored the moment while he could, knowing full well that it wouldn't last long. Once the wizard regained his composure, his mind would surely start working to solve the riddle of how the events of the day had led to the death of his friend.

Silently, George considered his next move. *What would be more devastating ... reclaiming the body of Edward's mother and using her frail body to extinguish her son's life, or reentering the wizard and steering the man to murder the woman who'd given birth to him? Decisions, decisions.* Finally making up his mind, George drifted toward the stable where he'd stored the old woman for safe keeping.

For the better part of the last hour, Edward had been

overcome with grief. Though the debilitating sadness he felt was far from over, his tear ducts had dried up, refusing to allow even the smallest trickle of moisture to leave their confines. Closing his eyes, he took a deep breath and slowly exhaled in an attempt to clear his mind. He was tempted to wipe the liquid sorrow from his dampened cheeks, but decided not to. Instead, he resolved to leave his tear stained face untouched. Sort of like wearing a badge of shame.

The hint of a warm breeze drifted through the open portal which led outside, turning cold for a second and causing a shiver to run up his spine as he turned his head toward the doorway. The feeling was so brief that it triggered a memory, one in which his mother was telling him a story when he was a child. Her words vaguely wafted through his mind. Something about a ghost walking over a grave. Shaking his head to clear the vision, Edward pushed himself up from the floor. Absently, he began pacing back and forth. Even once he realized what he was doing he didn't stop; he understood that his body was subconsciously forcing him through the motions because, for whatever reason, it helped clear his mind so he could think.

When he could no longer take the sound of the thickening blood on the floor squishing under his worn boots, a sickening reminder of his dead friend, he stopped and regarded the scattered pieces of Jack. *I should probably gather his remains and at least give him a decent burial,* he thought. It would have been bad enough to see his furry body parts strewn recklessly around the room, but somehow it was worse seeing the severed appendages littered about in their human appearance. Silently, he cursed the fact that werewolves reverted from their wolf form upon death. The task ahead would have at least been slightly easier if Edward could have convinced himself that he was burying a wild animal instead of a friend, and ally. Gathering what few remnants of resolve he had left, Edward turned and strode to the door, determined to honor Jack.

As he walked outside, he was greeted by the warm, afternoon sun. Immediately upon his exit from the inn, a murder of crows took flight, leaving only a few of their fellows dotting the corpse of his horse. One of them glanced toward Edward, a malevolent gleam in its beady black eyes, as if it were daring him to approach. When the enormous bird saw that its warning was being heeded, it returned to greedily feasting upon the horse's flesh, stretching a decayed piece of sinew from the animal's hide with its blood splattered beak.

Knowing the task ahead of him would not be an easy one, he did his best to ignore the foul creatures defiling his once proud steed and scoured the town in search of ground which was soft enough that he could move it with his bare hands. After canvassing nearly every square inch of the abandoned village, and not finding a suitable area to bury Jack, he resigned himself to collecting rocks. He had seen this interment tactic used before when there were no digging implements available, the object of which was to encase the body in stone so that wild animals would be less likely to ravage the corpse of the deceased. As Edward began toting rocks to the location he'd chosen to enshrine Jack's remains, a place between the inn and the structure beside it—which he had picked out because it received shade for the majority of the day—he heard a noise coming from within the building; the sound was reminiscent of a muffled voice. A female voice!

A gleeful madness twinkled in his eyes as George entered the stable. In the dimness of the interior, he floated toward his restrained victim. When his ghostly form drifted into the crone's field of vision, she tilted her bloodshot eyes in his direction. Though her wrinkled face was a shade somewhere between red and purple, most likely caused by her struggles and the rope encircling her neck, she uttered a muffled scream; the gag George had made from a strip of her gown wound tightly around her head, cutting painfully into her cheeks, successfully muted her cries of terror.

Knowing his time was short, he inched closer to Victoria. As he was about to slip inside her body and take control, her wide-eyed look of panicked hope distracted him. Something, or someone, was on the other side of the wall! For a moment he had almost dismissed the noise, but the old woman's reaction gave him reason to hurry.

Quickly, George slid into the fleshy disguise of Edward's mother and took control. The woman choked and gasped as he forced her to lean forward so he could remove the bindings. Throwing the loosened ropes to the side, he stood up. Within seconds of doing so the stable door flew open, sending the shadows of the interior into hiding as bright sunlight penetrated the gloom.

"Mother?" Edward rushed toward her, casting confused glances to each corner of the giant room as he approached. Stopping in front of her, he put his hands firmly on her arms and bent his head down slightly to meet her eyes. "Are you all right? I thought I heard screaming." Gently, he brushed her frazzled, gray hair from her features and searched her bloodshot, brown irises for an answer.

"I ... I think so," her cracked and aged voice finally responded, a bewildered expression etched on her face. She smoothed out her dirty and disheveled gown before meeting her son's gaze again. Without realizing he was doing it, George contorted Victoria's features into a frown. Edward's piercing stare told George that he didn't believe the words rolling off his mother's tongue.

Raising one hand, Edward brushed his fingertips across her cheek. "If everything is fine, then what are these marks? And while I'm thinking about it, what were you doing in here? Everyone in the inn thought you slipped out during the night to return to Elysia."

"I must have sleepwalked here because I have no memory of leaving the inn," George lied, hoping the excuse would be believable. Especially considering the fact he had no idea if it was something the woman had ever done before. "As for the marks ... they were probably caused by whatever I fell asleep on." As George studied the wizard's face he saw the worry lines begin to soften.

Not entirely satisfied with his mother's response, but enough so to put off any reservations he had, Edward turned back toward the open stable door and put an arm around her shoulder. As he stepped forward to lead her outside, he realized that there was unfinished business awaiting him. Business that his mother should not be forced to witness.

"Why are you stopping?" George tilted her head upward to see if he had somehow managed to put together the pieces and sensed there was something amiss.

Edward hesitated before answering, then looked down into her uplifted face. "There's something I must do," he began sadly, a tear slipping from the corner of one eye. "However, after finding you again, I am trying to figure out how," he continued. "I don't want to leave you alone, but I also don't want you to witness it." Sighing heavily, he chanced a look into her eyes. She appeared to be deep in thought.

Shrugging her shoulders, Victoria sidestepped from beneath his arm and plopped down on a musty bale of straw near the open door. "I'll just wait here for you. Is that a viable alternative?" Her lips pressed together in a tight-lipped smile and one eyebrow lifted questioningly.

As much as he hated to leave her somewhere that was not in his direct line of sight, Edward knew it was probably for the best. "I will try not to take too long." For a moment he considered forcing a promise out of her that she would stay put, but changed his mind when he realized it would likely have an unwanted affect. It would probably do one of two things: either it would offend her, or it would raise her curiosity. Neither of which were options he wished to explore right now.

Grudgingly, Edward turned his back on his mother as he strode toward the inn to retrieve the pieces of his dear friend in order to honor him with a decent burial. Behind him, a wicked grin creased Victoria's face.

Chapter 10

The raining debris from above them had stopped, and an eerie silence enveloped them for approximately an hour, maybe more. It was so quiet, in fact, that Katie felt it was like being a musician in a recording studio who was on a break in between tracks. She found herself wishing that a bird would squawk, a cricket would chirp ... something, anything to bring an end to the isolation she now felt, showing her they weren't the only living creatures left in the world.

As if Brian had been reading her thoughts, he whispered softly in her ear, "What do you think? Is it safe to come out of hiding and resume our journey?"

"I don't know," she replied, turning her head to regard him. "We should probably at least test the waters to see. I sure don't relish the thought of staying put until dark so we can sneak away in the shadows. My hand is already broken, I don't want to add any other fractured bones to my list of injuries."

Brian smirked as he attempted to restrain his laughter, exhaling a breathy snicker through his nose.

"I'm glad you find me so entertaining," she commented sarcastically. Katie desperately wanted to throw a hand on her hip to emphasize her point, but knew that if she did she would probably lose her balance and fall to her death. *Definitely not an option.*

"Sorry. Your plan is as good as any, if you ask me," he stated in a more serious tone. "Let me know when you're ready and I'll help you get back over to the rails."

She hesitated for a moment as she considered their options. *Why does he want me to go first?* The thought had no more than entered her mind when the answer came to her and she felt like smacking herself in the head for being dimwitted. At first she had pondered the possibility that he was sacrificing the weakest link, presenting the vulture of opportunity with a tasty morsel ... if said creature was still lurking about. Sure, it was a metaphor for Brian throwing her out first as bait, but it didn't seem quite as offensive to think of it that way. After a moment of indecision, she realized the true reasoning behind his words. *He feels safer about helping me to the tracks first than he does about him taking the lead and leaving me clinging to this tree trunk with a broken hand.* "I'm ready, I guess," she finally replied with a grim smile.

With an almost imperceptible nod, he slowly extended a leg toward the rails and scuffed his boot in the dirt to create a divot he could use to maintain his balance. Keeping one hand firmly wrapped around the trunk of the pine, he used his other to steady Katie. "Go ahead," he urged. "Step away from the tree and use my foot to brace yourself. Think of it as a stepping stone."

Following his instructions, she eased herself into position, allowing her body weight to shift backwards slightly. Once Katie felt secure enough to move, she stretched her leg toward the tracks. As she wedged her foot against Brian's boot, she began to panic, feeling his foot skid a couple of inches in the loose dirt. Forcing herself to hurry, worried that he would lose his footing, she swung her weight rapidly from his steadying hand to his boot and jumped the final few feet to the rail. As she reached out for its gleaming, metal surface, Katie realized there was a problem. The hand which grasped at the track was her broken one! She didn't hear Brian howl in agony as she pushed off from his extended leg; her own screams of pain drowned them out as she clutched desperately to the hot metal rail to keep herself from tumbling downhill. Tiny dots swirled before her eyes and her vision threatened to darken. Leaning forward, Katie dug her feet into the dirt just above one of the wooden support beams between the tracks, closed her eyes, and took a deep breath.

When she opened them, the world continued to swim for a few seconds, almost as if Katie had just returned home from a night on the town, on the precipice of being fall down drunk and hoping to find her bed before passing out. Once her vision became steadier, she glanced toward Brian and saw a grimace of concern on his face. "I'm all right," she assured him. "Let me get myself braced, then I'll help you cross over."

Frowning, he wondered how she could possibly help him in her condition. The last thing he wanted to do was put more strain on her broken hand, knowing the added pressure would be, at the very least, excruciating. Possibly even enough so to break her grip, which would cause both of them to tumble to the bottom of the incline and likely kill them. His worries began to subside when he figured out her plan. There was a slight gap between the underside of the rail and the ground beneath it, which she managed to squeeze her arm through, using it like a hook to hold herself in place. With her right foot wedged on top of the support beam between the tracks, Katie extended her left leg toward him. Scuffing the ground with her toes, she created a rut for her foot to keep herself steady. Then she reached out, splaying her fingers and indicating she was ready. "Come on," she urged.

Letting out the slow breath he hadn't realized he'd been holding, Brian stretched out his arm. Katie immediately latched on to his hand with a grip that felt like a vise, which surprised him for a moment. He hadn't expected her to be so capable; her slender frame obviously much stronger than it appeared. Feeling secure, he let go of the tree. Keeping his left foot in the groove he had made to support himself, he stepped toward her with his right, extending it outward and using hers as a stepping stone. Within moments he was safely across and clinging to her like a leech. Once he regained his balance, Brian moved to the right of Katie, occupying the other half of the support beam.

Watching expectantly from the shadows of a large boulder, Verin saw the duo come back into view as he gazed down the slope of hill bisected by the tracks. *Damn! It would have made life so much simpler if they had fallen. I could have gone back to work without worrying about the interruption of intruders, but now I'll have to take matters into my own hands.* Letting his breath out in a hiss, he floated down from his observation point and gathered the minions close.

Even though he wasn't their master, and they knew his orders did not hold any weight, the cluster of impish creatures turned their attention to Verin. Perhaps, if they followed his instructions, the Black Knight would show them favor in the future. Maybe even elevate their status among his legions.

Once Verin had their undivided attention, he took a quick peek over the boulder to check the intruders' progress. They were approaching much faster than he had anticipated. Turning to face the mass of expectant minions, he let out a low growl as he spoke. "I need all of you to do what you can to knock the interlopers down the hill. Hiding in the shadows is no longer an option. I don't care if you have to run down there and engage them, I want results this time!"

Though his form held no definitive shape, one thing became perfectly clear as the tiny creatures turned to do his bidding. The mist-like substance that made up his essence swirled into a twisted grin as Verin spun around, disappearing through the portal which led inside to Cemetery Hill.

After safely making it back to the railroad tracks, Brian and Katie resumed their climb. It wasn't long, a half an hour perhaps, before she began to notice a change in his breathing as she followed close on his heels. Reaching upward, she tugged on the hem of his pants to get his attention. He stopped immediately and turned to regard her. *I'm right!* Seeing the overcast glaze of his eyes as he gazed down at her caused Katie to realize they were not alone. "How bad is it? Can you tell?"

"Not for sure," he replied, shaking his head. "It feels sort of like the sense I was getting in the town below yesterday, right before we were attacked, but not nearly as strong."

"Well, we *did* greatly diminish their numbers before they fled," she reminded him.

"True."

"Do you think it could be the leftovers from yesterday's battle that you're feeling now?"

"I would say it's a distinct possibility," he confirmed, barely getting the words from his lips before a deluge of small, falling rocks cascaded down upon them and Katie caught sight of something moving above them.

She had no more than lifted a hand to shield her eyes from the debris raining down on them when the day suddenly became brighter. Squinting, Katie chanced a look toward Brian and discovered the reason behind the new brilliance. There was an outcropping of rock above them, hardly discernible because the shaman had ushered forth another of his gigantic, holy fires.

The sound of unearthly screams erupted from above, and as Katie watched on in horror, several dancing flames separated themselves from the conflagration. She was tempted to cover her ears to shut out the high-pitched wails of the tiny demons, but then noticed a few of them hopping erratically downhill toward them. "Brian, watch out!" she yelled to no avail. The shaman seemed to either not hear her or was unable to move out of the way. Six tiny balls of fire skittered dangerously close, but just as they were about to collide with Brian they exploded, plastering his face and clothing with a flaming green goo. Quickly scrambling to his side, Katie furiously patted out the fires with her hand before they had a chance to consume his clothes and sear his flesh.

Chapter 11

After gathering the scattered remnants of Jack's mutilated corpse, Edward turned and strode toward the door. Immediately, he was forced to stop in his tracks as his mother's frail form stood in the opening, blocking his exit. "Mother? What are you doing in here? I thought I asked you to stay in the stable." A scowl, partly out of frustration, but with a hint of anger, creased his weathered face. His penetrating glare did nothing to prompt an answer out of her. She continued to stand in his way, unmoving, as if she were rooted in place, offering him no explanation for her presence. Exhaling sharply, he stalked toward her. "I didn't want you to see this," he grumbled. "Will you please go back to the stable and stay there like I asked?"

Remaining fixed in place like a statue, a barely noticeable glow flickered in her soft, brown eyes giving them a goldish hue for a second or two. An imperceptible grin split her wrinkled cheeks as the scent of death, combined with the coppery smell of blood soaking into the floorboards, wafted into her nostrils. "I'm not going anywhere," she replied flatly as Edward stopped in front of her.

He felt his cheeks flush with anger as her hot breath washed over his skin, and nearly turned to find an alternate exit from the inn, but suddenly something didn't feel right to him. Thoughts swirled through his mind as Edward quickly tried to work out the problem. Then, it hit him. *Her breath! It felt like a warm, summer breeze, but not in a good way. It carried the stench of death and decay in its wake, like wind blowing through a graveyard.* An awful memory surfaced, one that he had hoped was behind him. A vision of the time he had spent on future Earth, fighting for survival in a world that was populated with flesh eating zombies. *That's what her breath smelled like! The stench of rotted flesh!* Instinctively, bile rose in the back of his throat.

Seeing the pale, sickly pallor of Edward's face caused a wicked grin to emerge on her countenance, making Victoria look like the scheming devil that was intertwined with her soul. Her eyes flashed brightly, emitting a demonic radiance that reflected off of her son's pasty flesh. Stepping forward while Edward was confused and disoriented, George raised her arms. Her brittle, aged digits encircled her son's throat and began to squeeze.

Caught by surprise, he dropped Jack's remains to the floor and his piercing gray eyes bulged in shocked disbelief. He lifted his hands and grabbed her arms in an attempt to break her grip, which was considerably stronger than he would have ever expected. Especially from an old, arthritic woman! At first Edward's attempts seemed futile; he could feel her fingernails biting into his flesh. Warm liquid trickled down his neck, which he somehow knew wasn't the sweat of exertion, but blood. His vision began to fade in and out, much like it had when he was battling the horde of tiny demons yesterday, and he was on the verge of blacking out. Unable to break the vise-like hold his mother had on him, Edward realized he didn't have much longer. Though, he did wonder why she was acting like this. "Why?" he wheezed, trying to catch a breath, his eyeballs beginning to bulge in their sockets.

The inflection that responded was not his mother's. "Because you're in my way," a hollow male voice intoned, Victoria's lips parting to reveal a malicious smile. "Well, that and I rather enjoy watching you suffer. Seeing your life vanish as if it were a wisp of smoke will be priceless."

His struggles grew more intense when it occurred to him that his mother wasn't in control of her body. *That explains why her breath smelled so foul! There is an evil spirit inside of her, pulling her strings like a puppeteer! The stench of decay coming from her mouth should have been my first clue,* he silently berated himself, wishing now that he hadn't sent Brian and Katie away. The shaman could likely have expelled the malignant spirit. Redoubling his efforts, Edward lashed out and punched with every ounce of strength he could muster. When his fist collided with her wrinkled face he felt like crying. There was no time for that now, though. The force of the impact had accomplished its goal. Victoria released her grip on his throat, raising her hands to her face as she staggered backwards.

It only took George a moment to regroup, while Edward appeared to be appalled by his own actions. Shaking her head to clear the cobwebs, which was difficult to do in someone so old, he piloted her body toward him. Forgetting that there was a cluster of scattered limbs sprawled across the floorboards between them, she lost her balance and tumbled forward. As she landed with a sickening splat, Edward jumped backwards and slipped on the blood soaked boards beneath his feet. His arms pinwheeled for a split second, but this only caused him to overbalance and fall forward instead of crashing to the floor on his rear end. The sound of Victoria falling on top of Jack had made him sick to his stomach, but when his body landed on top of hers he heard the crunch of bone beneath him, which was far worse.

After a few failed attempts, his fingers slipping and sliding on the blood-slicked floor, Edward managed to skitter off of the heap. Sitting a couple of feet away and breathing in ragged gasps, he eyed the mound of flesh for movement. Victoria didn't move right away, but before Edward could decide his next course of action she appeared to be coming out of her daze. Trying to boost herself to a sitting position, she pushed against the bloody floorboards with one withered hand. Her attempts were no more successful than Edward's had been as her arm buckled and shot out from beneath her, causing her to tilt forward too fast and lose her precarious balance. The sound of her jaw smacking into the boards, her fragile jawbones breaking on impact, resonated from the walls of the empty inn. The echo of which made Edward cringe.

Tenderly rubbing her jaw, Victoria raised her head and locked her soft brown eyes on Edward in agonized disbelief. A bloodied strand of her gray hair swung before her like a frayed windshield wiper, leaving tiny crimson smears on her wrinkled cheeks. Inwardly though, George was grinning from ear to ear, knowing that it wouldn't take much to push the wizard far enough to finish the job.

For the briefest of moments, Edward admired the resilience of his mother. This thought was pushed aside when reality grabbed hold of him again; Victoria reached out for him as if asking 'Why did you do this to me?' then slapped her hand in the growing puddle of blood between them, hooking her fingertips into the floorboards and clawing her way closer.

Scrambling for a viable solution to his dilemma, ideas swirled through Edward's mind with the ferocity of a tornado. The mere contemplation of most of them turned his stomach. *I can't! She's my mother!* While outwardly these thoughts had merit, Edward knew Victoria was no longer in control of her own body. *It's that spirit ... or demon inside of her that is making her act this way,* he considered angrily, desperately wishing Brian was here to back him up. If I don't figure something out, and quick, I won't have to worry about doing the unthinkable to her. She will do it to me!

Another hand slapped the floor. A few more inches and she would be able to latch on to him. He scooted back a couple of feet to stay out of her reach, giving himself extra time to think. Then it hit him! Feeling like an idiot for not considering it sooner, he backed away even more and closed his eyes, concentrating. A bluish glow, faint at first but rapidly growing in intensity, enveloped his scarred hands.

Even from this distance, George felt the drop in ambient air temperature which had begun in synchronization with the blue light emanating from the wizard's hands. *This is it,* he thought, preparing to depart the body of his host. He would have to time it perfectly in order to get to safety so he could have a front row seat to the slaughter.

Just as Edward was about to unleash his spell, a flicker of movement near the doorway distracted his attention. At first he had thought it was his imagination playing tricks on him—it had done that quite frequently in the last twenty four hours—but within seconds he knew it wasn't a hallucination this time. The ghostly form of Amber materialized in the shadows to the left of the opening. Panic, or perhaps terror, permeated her features.

"Don't do it, Edward! It's a trick!" Amber's horrified voice screeched and her transparent form began to pulsate rapidly.

"I have to," he told her with a pained expression. "It will give Brian the time to return and take care of this matter properly."

Victoria continued to claw her way across the slippery boards toward her son, her eyes flitting from her son to the intruder as if she were watching a tennis match. *Just a couple more seconds.* Edward was turning his attention back to her as she made one final, desperate lunge. Her bony fingers clamped on to the toe of his boot. Glancing up at the wizard in triumph, her eyes bulged in horror. The bluish light emanating from Edward's hands seemed to crackle with energy and George knew in a matter of moments his opportunity to flee would be gone. Quickly, he forced his presence from her body, creating a gust of wind that Edward was unlikely to notice, probably thinking it was caused by his magic. He stood in the doorway for a minute as he looked back with pleasure.

His ghostly form, unlike Amber's, was masked from sight by the late day sunlight filtering through the opening. A wicked smile played across his lips as he glanced down at the old woman, who was now nothing more than a block of ice.

Chapter 12

The sunlight was rapidly fading from the day and the holy fire Brian had torched the demons with was nearly burned out. Amid the tortured screams of the creatures, the two of them had held their position, allowing the flames to do their work. If it had been up to Katie, however, they would have rushed toward the outcropping of rock above them as soon as the shaman's eyes had cleared. It didn't seem fair that Brian had shouldered the burden of eradicating the tiny demons. She wanted to have a hand in it as well, feeling it would have given her a sense of vengeance and retribution for what the creatures had done to Edward.

Once the two of them had deemed it safe, they began to climb again. It didn't take nearly as long as either of them had thought to reach the ledge. They stood at the edge of the precipice for a few minutes to catch their breath, idly tamping out the lingering flames with their boots.

"Yuck!" Katie dry heaved as her foot squished down on a combination of melted flesh, bone, and sticky, green blood. She threw a hand up over her mouth. The stench of cooked flesh had been bad before, but after stepping in the aftermath of the massacre the odor was even more overpowering. Moving a few feet away, she scuffed the sole of her boot on the rocky ground to remove most of the goo and gore.

"Check it out," Brian remarked, the comment distracting her from the wretched task of cleaning her boot.

With a grim expression, she turned to look. He was pointing at the railroad tracks they had been following until now. Katie studied them briefly, noticing the sharp curve of the rails as they crested the hill to where she stood, then followed their path for a short distance. When she saw the termination point a couple of hundred feet away, she gasped loudly. "Please, tell me I'm not seeing things," she breathed excitedly. "Did we really find the end? Please tell me that dark spot over there is not a tunnel going through the mountain."

"I don't think it is. It looks more like a cave than anything," Brian confided.

"I hope you're right." She smiled. Katie was so happy she felt like skipping toward it as if she were playing a game with Julie when they were much younger. The thought of her lost friend caused her to pause, her mood quickly shifting to sadness as she realized it had been too long since she had thought about Julie. *How can I forget about her? Everything I've been doing since coming to this crazy world has been to find her!*

"Why'd you stop?" Brian gazed at her in confusion, noticing the tears forming in the corners of her eyes.

"Sorry," she mumbled, wiping away the liquid sadness with her fingertips and forcing a weak smile.

Closing the distance between them, Brian wrapped an arm around her shoulders in a brief hug. Gently lifting her chin, he looked into her puffy brown eyes. "Cheer up.

With any luck this will all be over with soon and we can get back to town to check on Edward." As soon as the words left his mouth, Brian realized that he might have been wrong about the reasons behind her mood.

"I want to say that it isn't Edward I'm worried about ... that he's a big boy and can take care of himself, but that would be a lie." She paused for a second to collect her thoughts, then continued, "Sure, I'm worried about Edward, but it was my friend, Julie, that I was just thinking about."

Brian seemed to consider this for a few moments, as if he didn't know who she was talking about. "The girl that we were traveling with back on Earth? The one that turned out to be a machine?"

"Yes."

Now he understood why she felt the way she did. Back when they were on Earth, Katie had thought she had been reunited with her friend, only to have the feeling swept from beneath her feet like a rug. He couldn't begin to imagine the devastation she had felt when she found out the truth, or the underlying depression because the evil of this world had toyed with her emotions and led her astray. "Let's go find out what's in that cave," he whispered, grasping her hand softly and urging her forward, trying his best to get her mind off the subject.

She shuffled her feet, unwillingly at first, in his wake as he led her toward the dark oval set in the side of the mountain. As they drew nearer she began to notice the cadence of Brian's breathing changing slightly. "Is everything okay?" Katie tugged lightly on his hand to get his attention. When he turned to face her, she saw no difference in his bright blue eyes. They weren't clouding over as they did when something really bad was about to happen.

"I ... I think so," he stammered, unsure of himself. "I can sort of feel something, but I can't make out what it is."

Just ahead, there was a platform rail-car occupying the tracks. It appeared to be sitting alone, like a silent sentinel, guarding the entrance of the cave. Keeping a wary eye on and around the platform, as if they expected some sort of ambush, they skirted around the car and approached the opening. Little did they know that the ease of their entry was facilitated by Verin, forgetting to close the chamber off from the outside world. If they had known, they might have even thanked him for his stupidity, though probably not until after they had killed him.

As the two of them stepped through the opening, a strange, red luminescence fell over their vision like a veil of blood. "What the ..." Brian began. "Why couldn't we see this weird light from outside the cave?"

"I have no idea," Katie replied. It took a minute for their eyes to adjust. Even though there was light inside the cave, it was a much darker color than the lingering daylight outside. Katie inhaled sharply when her vision became accustomed to the difference. She looked around in shocked horror, suddenly realizing it was not a cave they were in, but a large chamber. Her chin dropped so far it nearly touched her chest. "Holy ... fucking ... shit!"

Greeting her in the dim redness was row after row of tall, wooden crosses, like an odd graveyard. Or perhaps, a crucifixion chamber. Shackles were dangling from either side of the crossbars and another set was attached near the base of each fixture. A strange, metal object, which looked like a remnant from an electric chair execution, rested against the frame just above the crosspiece. Every cross seemed to be similarly retrofitted. Though most of them lay idle and barren, there were some, randomly throughout the room, that had nude prisoners attached to them.

Katie's eyes suddenly transformed, gleaming with excitement. "I wonder ..." Her words broke off as she realized the possibility that this could be the place where Julie was being held captive. Quickly, she wove her way between the crosses, affording a brief glance toward each prisoner she encountered. Halfway across the expansive chamber, she stopped dead in her tracks. "Oh my God! Julie!" Tears, both of anguish and elation, streamed down her cheeks as if the dam which held them in place had been smashed to pieces. "Brian! Come quick!"

The shaman rushed to her side. He had already been moving toward her at a brisk pace after hearing Katie yell out her friend's name, but hurried his stride further when he heard the urgency in her voice. Stopping next to her, he averted his eyes from the captive and kept them focused on Katie; his priestly vows from his days back on Earth making it extremely difficult to gaze on the girl's nude body. The mere thought of it seemed like it would be a sin. Not to mention the age difference, which would make Brian feel like a pedophile.

Surveying the implements that held Julie in place, Katie's eyes darted from one binding to the next. She stepped forward and bent down to study the shackles which held her friend's ankles. *How are we going to get these things off of her? We obviously don't have a key to unlock these fucking cuffs!* Katie let out a heavy sigh of despair when she saw the keyhole embedded in the metal, then stood back up and turned to Brian. "Can you boost me up, so I can see if there's a way to remove that thing on her head?"

For a few seconds, he considered the best way to help Katie. Then Brian turned his back to the naked girl and cupped his hands in front of him, locking his fingers together as tightly as he could manage. He didn't even get a chance to nod to her that he was ready. Before his head could move an inch, she had her left hand on his shoulder and one of her feet in the makeshift stirrup and was pulling herself up.

Once the contraption on Julie's head was at eye level, Katie noticed a small bundle of wires were attached to the back side of the helmet. Following their path with a studious gaze, she saw the tiny strands disappear in the darkness above her, probably running along the ceiling to some unknown power source. Tilting her head slightly, she inspected the area where the cluster of wires joined the helm. Leaning forward to brace herself, Katie positioned the bundle against the wood of the upper section of the cross with her broken hand. Reaching down with the other, she loosened the short sword from the belt at her side and drew it. Being in her non-dominant hand, the blade felt unnatural in her grip, almost unwieldy. Raising it above her head, she prepared to strike. The hilt wobbled slightly as she swung, but her blow landed precisely where she had intended. A brief shower of sparks cascaded down as the connection was severed and the frayed copper brushed across the blade.

Almost immediately, as if someone had flicked on a light switch, Julie's eyelids fluttered open. She quickly scrunched them closed. Even the dim lighting of the chamber hurt her eyes. Carefully, she opened them again, but only a slit. Once they began to adjust, Julie blinked them fully open. To her surprise, the first thing she saw was Katie's smiling face. Julie tried to speak, but only a rush of air escaped her lips, almost as if her vocal cords had forgotten how they were supposed to work. *Oh well,* she thought. *At least Katie found me.*

Her eyes bulged in panic as she attempted to throw her arms around Katie and realized she couldn't move. Putting a hand to Julie's cheek, Katie caressed it gently. "Shhh. It'll be okay. Brian and I will get you out of here," she whispered reassuringly, hoping to calm her friend.

Once Julie stopped thrashing around in an attempt to free herself, Katie studied the bindings that held her friend's arms outstretched. There was a very short section of chain attached to the cuff encircling Julie's wrist, the opposite end of which was bolted in to the wooden crossbar. Upon further inspection of the individual links, Katie thought it might be possible to hack through them in the same manner she had used to sever the wires of the helmet. The biggest problem would be not whacking off her friend's hand in the process. Knowing the likelihood was slim that she would be able to deliver a strike that would free Julie, and not disable her, Katie climbed down from her perch.

"Can you try to cut through her chains?" Katie's eyes pleaded with Brian as she offered the sword to him.

With great hesitation, he took the blade from her. He closed his eyelids and inhaled deeply, wishing he could make the girl invisible, and exhaled loudly through his pursed lips as he reopened them. Turning toward the naked girl he bent down, deciding to attempt removing the least objectionable bindings first. Moving his head from one side to the other, Brian realized it was not going to be an easy task. The gap between her ankles was negligible, having only two links separating the cuffs. The back side of the metal bands would be slightly easier, but more work. Each of them were affixed to the base of the cross with their own chain, meaning there was twice the opportunity to screw up. Knowing what had to be done, Brian glanced up at Katie. "Grab onto her ankles and pull them away from the cross," he instructed.

Kneeling down beside him, she clamped her hands around the cool metal and did as she was told. Once the chains were tight, he raised the sword. Taking a deep breath to steady his hands, he brought the blade down with careful swiftness. Sparks jumped as metal met metal, but the chain remained intact. With one hand, he extended his fingertips to see if his efforts had yielded any results at all. Pulling his arm back with a sharp inhalation of breath, he stuck his index finger in his mouth.

"Anything?" Katie inquired.

"I must have nicked it. There was a sharp barb on one of the links," he admitted.

"That sounds hopeful." She smiled. "Keep at it. I'll do my best to make sure her legs don't get in the way."

With a nod, he brought the blade up to try again. After several attempts, he finally managed to hack through both of the chains. Readjusting his position, Brian took another deep breath, knowing the section between the girls ankles was going to be even more difficult to pull off without someone getting hurt.

Seeing the doubt in his eyes, Katie gently patted his back. "It's all right, Brian. I have faith that your aim will be true," she whispered, hoping to bolster his confidence.

"I'm not sure I can do this," he replied, shaking his head. "I'm afraid of missing my mark. Surely you don't want me to lop her foot off."

Seeing heavy beads of sweat on his brow, she encouraged him in the only way she could. "You have a much better chance of success than I do." She held up her broken hand to punctuate her point. "I wouldn't be able to wield the sword with enough strength to do the job, and I'm sure you would have a better chance of keeping the blade steady."

Letting out the mother of all sighs, Brian closed his eyelids and tried to envision the blow in his mind. When he opened his eyes, the look in his piercing blue irises was focused. Determined not to let Katie down, he wiped the sweat from his forehead on his sleeve. Gripping the hilt tightly in both hands, he raised the sword and said a quick, silent prayer. Miraculously, when the blade came down the links between the cuffs broke free, separating as if he were Moses parting the Red Sea. His held breath rushed from his lungs in relief. "I did it!" He turned his grateful eyes on Katie, knowing he would have never had the courage to deliver the strike without her.

"I knew you could," she smiled broadly. "Two to go, then we can get out of this wretched place."

Feeling more confident now, Brian stood. As he glanced up toward Julie's bound wrists, his smile faltered. The chains which held her arms in place were similar to those that had prohibited her from kicking her feet away from the cross. Even if he could manage a clear shot, the angle would be awkward and it would force him to take something off the blow. Otherwise, the risk of amputating her arm would be too great.

Noticing the nervous expression blooming on Brian's face, she glanced upward and saw what he was worrying about. Katie quickly came up with a solution and dropped to all fours, keeping as much pressure off of her broken hand as she could. The look on the shaman's face softened when he realized her intentions. "Are you sure? What about your …"

"Don't worry about me," she interrupted. "Climb up. I'll keep as steady as I can."

Placing a tentative foot on her back, he gradually increased the pressure as he shifted his weight onto her. Taking a quick peek down, he saw she hadn't even flinched, which made him grateful that he was skinny. Refocusing his attention on the task before him, he noticed the angle of his strike would be considerably more favorable.

After several attempts to hack through the chains that held Julie in place upon the cross, first one arm, then the other, fell to her side as Brian freed her. The shackles around her ankles and wrists remained, but since they were no longer attached to the wooden cross her feet were firmly planted on the ground and she could move about normally. Hopping down from his perch, Brian bent and helped Katie to stand.

It took a few seconds for Julie's freedom to register in her mind. Their brown eyes locked onto each other, partially in disbelief. Katie threw her arms around Julie, pulling her in to a tight embrace, tears gushing freely down her cheeks. "I can't believe I finally found you," Katie whispered in her ear, relieved that the ordeal was over. Ever since her departure from her home on Earth, Katie had felt as if a part of herself was missing, perhaps even dead.

Brian stood a short distance from them, his lips stretched into a broad grin. Helping the two girls to reunite made him feel better than he had in a long time. It was one thing to use his shamanic or priestly powers to aid his friends, but somehow the sight before him was more satisfying because he had brought them together the old-fashioned way. As he watched the two of them cling to each other, his brow furrowed in confusion. The look in the newly freed girl's eyes was one of panic, or perhaps terror, as she rested her chin on Katie's shoulder. *She should be overcome with joy, not looking like she's scared.* "What's wrong?" He took a step toward the girls, directing his question to Julie.

His inquiry startled Katie. She loosened her hold on Julie and turned her head to look at Brian. "What do you mean? Now that we are together again, nothing is wrong."

Without speaking, Julie nervously turned her attention to the corner of the expansive chamber, pointing toward a large, black oval with a shaky finger.

Tearing his pale blue eyes away from Katie, he glanced in the direction the blonde girl pointed to. At first he only saw the blackened shape, which was slightly larger than a man, but as he continued to concentrate on the anomaly Brian began to hear an underlying hum of energy. There was something else, too. Faint sounds emanated from the blackness. Familiar things that reminded him of Earth, only they were muffled; almost as if he had cotton balls stuffed in his ears to block out the noise.

Noticing that Brian was no longer focused on her, Katie spun her head around to see what he was looking at. Seeing the oval void for the first time, a violent shiver crept up her spine. Even so, she started to move closer to inspect it. If her hunch was correct, it was a portal. The only question was ... where did it lead?

"Don't go near it!" Brian raised his voice when he saw Katie moving toward the strange blackness. "I'm sensing something bad." He had no more than spoken his warning when the shape began to shift. Oddly enough, it reminded him of a giant vagina, preparing to expel a newborn child. "We have to get out of here! Now!"

Hearing his urgent tone, Katie whipped her head around in time to see Brian grab hold of Julie's trembling hand and begin pulling her toward the exit. Rushing to catch up, her feet willed her away from the contorted portal despite her curiosity of what lay on the other side. "What's the hurry?"

"I have a feeling that something is about to emerge from whatever that thing is. I don't think it would be very wise to stick around and find out what that something is," he replied, his voice laced with worry.

As they approached the opening they had entered through, Brian hesitated. In the dim illumination of the chamber he saw a small control panel mounted on the wall to his left, near the exit. Quickly inspecting the labels around the various buttons and switches, he realized their purpose.

"Take your friend outside and climb aboard the rail-car," he instructed. "I think one of these buttons will power it up."

Julie didn't need any further encouragement. She stumbled toward the platform as fast as her unsteady legs would allow, but it was no easy task. Her limbs were still tingling as if they were asleep, which wasn't surprising. Especially considering that it had been a long time since she'd used them. Katie scrambled after her, then quickly boosted Julie to the surface of the platform.

Nervously, Brian glanced from the rail-car to the pulsing void, hoping they would have time to make their escape before something emerged from the darkness. When he saw the girls climb aboard, he pushed a button on the console. Immediately, a new hum carried to his ears from outside. Hurrying, he ran toward the platform and vaulted himself onto the smooth, wooden surface. He was very surprised that he had managed this feat on the first try, considering he had never been the athletic type.

Seconds ticked by and nothing happened. The rail-car vibrated softly beneath them, but so far it hadn't moved an inch. Initially, Brian had felt the hum of electricity building in intensity, but after a few moments the sensation had leveled off. On the edge of panic, he cast a nervous glance back toward the portal. Nothing had come out … yet, but he was sure if they dallied much longer that it would no longer be the case. *I've got to be missing something!* Quickly, he surveyed the platform. Spotting a lever near the front of the car, he scurried toward it, feeling like an idiot for not looking for an on-board control sooner. Being completely unfamiliar with trains and how to operate them—heck, he had never even had a model train as a youngster—he prepared to yank the lever. "If you can find something to hold on to, I would do it now if I were you," he yelled back to the girls.

Finding no handholds of any type, Katie scooted to the side of the platform and gripped the metal lip protruding from the outer edge. Instead of trying to do the same thing, Julie clung to her friend. With a nod of her head, Katie let Brian know they were as ready as they would ever be.

Closing his eyes, Brian let out a sharp breath then jerked the lever backward. The platform lurched forward like a roller coaster climbing its initial rise before dropping down the first incline. The only difference was the sickening crunch of bones beneath the large, metal wheels, and the disgusting squishes of the liquefied corpses of the tiny, demonic creatures littering their path.

After a few seconds, the rail-car nearly threw them from the platform as it rounded the first corner. The three of them took a collective breath of relief when they noticed they were all still aboard. Their temporary elation was interrupted moments later as the car tilted forward at a steep angle and they began to plummet down the hill.

Chapter 13

So far, there was no indication that the younger version of George would carry out his demands. The Black Knight had waited impatiently near the top of the stairs, masking himself in the shadows of the house's upper floor. As the first hints of a new day began to lighten the window at the end of the hall, the demon growled his contempt. *I'm beginning to think this may have been a fool's errand,* he thought, slowly drifting downstairs and contemplating an alternative solution. He stopped in the main hallway on the first floor, throwing a hesitant gaze between the front door and the bookcase that masked the stairway leading to George's secret torture chamber, trying to make up his mind. Blowing out a long breath through his clenched teeth, the Black Knight decided he would give George one last chance. "You better not fail me this time," he muttered as he slipped into the hidden passage. "If you do, it will be you who dies."

The incessant bray of the alarm clock on the nightstand awoke George. Reaching over to silence it before the foul thing gave him a headache, he missed the button. Instead of turning the alarm off, he succeeded in knocking the clock to the floor, causing it to buzz erratically and sound like a malfunctioning robot. The temptation to sit up and crush it under his foot was almost overpowering, but he closed his eyes for a moment to calm himself before bending forward to pull the cord from the wall. The ensuing silence was bliss to his head. Normally he woke in the morning with a caffeine withdrawal headache, and today was no different. Usually he could turn off the alarm fast enough that it didn't aggravate his throbbing brain, but not this time. The extended wailing of the alarm made his head hurt so much that he was nauseous.

Hopping up from the mattress and making a beeline to the bathroom, Jen noticed her husband sitting on the edge of the bed, pressing his fingers firmly against his closed eyes. "Are you all right?" Moving closer, she put a hand on his shoulder.

"Not really." He grimaced, her voice sounding as if she were yelling at him, even though he knew she wasn't. "Can you grab some aspirin for me on your way back from the bathroom?"

"Sure, baby. I'll be right back." Before leaving the room she bent down and kissed the top of his head lightly.

When her soft footsteps faded into the hallway, he opened his eyes a crack and swung his legs back onto the mattress. He almost kicked his sleeping daughter because he had forgotten she had spent the night in their bed. Leaning forward, he placed a hand on her side and gently shook her. "Wake up, sleepyhead."

With a yawn so wide it looked as if her jaws had unhinged like a snake devouring its prey, Cassie rubbed her eyes and attempted a smile. "Morning, Daddy," she mumbled. Blinking her eyelids to help her focus, she glanced into her father's pained face. Her happy expression evaporated when she realized she wasn't in her own room. "Why am I in here?"

"You had a nightmare, sweetie. Don't you remember?" Peering at her face, George could almost see the wheels turning in her head as she tried to recall the memory.

Suddenly, her pale blue eyes seemed to bulge in their sockets, her eyebrows looked as if they were scaling her forehead to hide under her mop of blonde hair, and her bottom jaw fell open. "The scary clown," she whispered in a frightened tone, as if she thought talking about it would somehow cause the monster to reappear.

"You want to know what I think?" Cassie nodded her head hesitantly. "I think it was that little boy who came in to use the bathroom last night. He was wearing a clown outfit. I think his name was Bradley, or something like that."

Now she shook her head vigorously, her blonde locks flinging wildly. "It wasn't Brady, Daddy. It was a monster!"

"Sweetie ... monsters aren't real," he lied, wondering if the creature he spoke to last night was still hanging around. He hoped it had left, but he would have to check the house after Cassie went to school and Jen went to work.

As if the mere thought of his wife had summoned her, Jen held out her hand and dropped a couple of aspirin into his palm. Grabbing the partial bottle of Mountain Dew from his nightstand, George popped the pills in his mouth and washed them down, hoping the caffeine in the beverage would speed the effectiveness of the medicine. "Thanks, baby," he smiled, wiping his chin with the back of his hand.

Reaching out, Jen grasped her daughter's hand and pulled her toward the edge of the bed. "Let's go, pumpkin. Time to get ready for school." She hesitated in the doorway, turning to face George for a second. "I'll start the coffee pot in a minute."

"No rush. I don't think I'm going to go to work today. I feel like crap."

With a thin smile, Jen turned away and led Cassie to her room.

His wife and daughter had left the house a couple of hours ago and the infusion of coffee was beating his headache into submission. Feeling better and having the place to himself, he allowed his thoughts to wander. Perhaps he would finally be able to take care of the unfinished business in the basement. It wasn't exactly his style to keep one of his victims hanging around for such a long period, but with all the free time he would have while his family was away, he would have ample opportunity to rectify the situation.

Draining the last of the coffee from his mug, he set the cup on the kitchen counter. Less than a minute later he was walking into the space behind the secret panel disguised as a bookshelf and descending the stone steps to his torture chamber.

Methodically, he opened and closed, first the outer

door, then the inner panel. Both were constructed of thick steel with a core of styrofoam, designed to muffle the sounds from the secret room and keep them from reaching other areas of the house. As he stepped into the chamber, closing the door behind him, George sensed something was wrong. The single, bare light bulb in the room cast eerie shadows in every corner, but that wasn't what bothered him. The bulb was only there to conveniently afford him a view of his victims, the fixture hanging from the ceiling directly above the place where his current prisoner was chained in place.

Tilting his head curiously, George realized something was different about the woman. He scanned her naked body in an attempt to determine what was not as it should be. His eyes roamed over her body, starting at her feet and drifting up her slender legs, noting that the shackles around her ankles were still firmly attached. As his gaze moved over her torso, his eyes settled on her bountiful bosom. He couldn't help himself; he had a thing for big breasted women. Saliva rapidly began to form in his mouth at the thought of ravishing the woman before he killed her, but then his mouth suddenly became as dry as a desert. *Her boobs should be heaving with each frightened breath she takes, but they're just hanging there lifelessly!* Quickly, his eyes darted upward and that's when he noticed her gag and blindfold had been removed.

Suddenly unsure of himself, George took a hesitant step toward his prisoner. As he got closer, he knew it was not a trick. The sickly greenish-blue pallor of her flesh reminded him of the dead woman in the bathtub scene from *The Shining*. As absurd as the thought was, the expression on her face suggested that she had been scared to death. Anger began to boil underneath the surface of his mind, suddenly feeling as if he'd been robbed of the ultimate pleasure of ending the woman's life.

A low growl formed in his throat as his rage continued to grow, but it was quickly silenced. The woman's eyes suddenly sprang open. The whites of them were now cloudy and yellowed, as well as bloodshot, and her pupils seemed to have swallowed her irises, making her eyes look black. As George took a backward step, the woman's mouth swung open. The foul stench of decay wafting from the orifice brushed against his cheek like a lover's kiss.

"You have one last chance to do my bidding," the corpse hissed, its swollen organ lolling from its mouth like an overstuffed sausage, split in the middle like a serpent's tongue.

"W-w-what if I refuse?" George stammered, taking another step back.

The Black Knight forced the corpse's cracked lips into a hideous grin. "Then you will share the fate of the pathetic creature before you."

The demonic entity's warning weighed heavily on his mind for the remainder of the day. A brooding silence surrounded George that neither Jen or Cassie could lift. After several failed attempts, his wife threw her hands in the air in exasperation and sighed. "Fine. Don't tell me what's bothering you, then!" Her frustrated tone was borderline hostile as she got up from the dinner table and stormed out of the room. Pouting, with tears forming in her eyes, Cassie quietly hopped down from her chair and slipped upstairs to her bedroom. The vacant expression on her father's face gave her the impression that he was upset about something. She hoped whatever was causing his silence was not her fault.

An hour passed before George was finally able to shake off the daze. Rubbing his temples, he exhaled softly as he saw the half eaten plates of food. Taking a thoughtful bite of his own dinner, though he wasn't really hungry, he spat it back onto his fork with a grimace. *How long have I been sitting here?* Normally he loved it when Jen cooked for him, but his dinner was now cold and tasted horrible.

Pushing his plate away in disgust, he turned his head toward the hallway and cocked it slightly. Straining to hear the voices of his family, the only sound he heard was that of the fall breeze outside, the winds causing the gutters to scrape and rattle against the side of the house. As George scooted his chair away from the table in preparation to check on Jen and Cassie, the Black Knight's warning resounded in his skull with the echoing intensity of a church bell in the fog. "Kill them, or suffer my wrath," the voice boomed, causing George to cringe.

As the words faded from his mind, he turned his red-rimmed eyes toward the kitchen window. The wind outside continued to pick up, blowing dead leaves and debris against the window panes. To George, the tiny scratching sounds were like fingernails on a chalkboard. Rising from his chair, he quickly exited the room and left the noise behind before it drove him mad.

His footsteps thumped heavily upon the carpeted stairs as he made his way to the second floor. As he attained the landing, he turned to climb the final few steps and saw Jen standing at the top with her hands on her hips. An angry fire seemed to light her normally soft, blue eyes. "Did you finally decide that you're ready to talk?" Her harsh tone gave her words a venomous quality, as if she were a viper about to strike.

Glancing up to meet her gaze, George tried to look as innocent and passive as he could manage. "I'm sorry, baby. I had a lot on my mind. I didn't mean to ignore you earlier," he apologized, unsure if what he said had any real bearing on the current situation. *Hell, for all I know, it could have been something else that set her off.*

Her piercing glare softened, but only a fraction. She seemed to be contemplating his words, as if she were lightly swishing a fine wine in her mouth to savor every nuance of its flavor. It was nearly a minute later when Jen finally spoke again. There was still a tense edge to her words, but they were nothing compared to the hostility and sarcasm she first addressed him with. "I forgive you, but you really *do* need to tell me what's bothering you." She eyed his expression as he climbed the remaining steps, then took his hand in hers and led him toward their bedroom.

Restless and unable to sleep, George rolled his head toward his lightly snoring wife. Though his pillow partially blocked his view, a sliver of moonlight from the bedroom window illuminated the part of her face that wasn't buried beneath her dark, wavy hair. She looked peaceful, which made what he knew he must do that much harder to fathom. He loved her dearly, or perhaps the idea of love was an endearing notion he could only hope to achieve in his lifetime, but had made up a story about what was bothering him to quell her anger. As repulsive as the thought was, deep down inside him George knew what he had to do. The Black Knight had forced his hand, putting him into survival mode. Kill, or be killed.

Turning his gaze toward the ceiling, he saw shadows dancing across its stark white surface; the moonlight filtering through the barren oak in the front yard causing them to appear as withered arms, flailing before his eyes as if they were reaching out for him. Closing his eyelids, George tried to block them out. *Out of sight, out of mind.* Trying to convince himself that this old mantra would work, he soon discovered otherwise. Even with his eyes shut tightly he could feel the shadows attempting to scratch their way into his mind.

Frustrated that he couldn't block them out of his head, George opened his eyelids. The disfigured shapes, which had crept across the ceiling moments ago, were gone. For a few seconds he considered the idea that he might have dreamed they were there in the first place, but he didn't honestly believe that.

The Black Knight's seething voice suddenly hissed in his head. "It's time." George clapped his hands over his ears as if he could mute the sound, but was rewarded with the demon's cackling laughter ricocheting through his mind. Emitting a soft sigh, he swung his legs over the side of the bed, knowing there was only one way to shut the foul creature up.

Quietly, he crossed the room to the partially open closet. Sweat began to dot his brow as he grasped the knob, hoping the door would not creak as he pulled it open. Noiselessly it swung wide, the ambient light in the room glinting off the object leaning against the back wall. Gathering his resolve, George reached for the cold steel of the Mossberg, pump action, 12 gauge shotgun. Soundlessly, he plucked the weapon from its resting place and cradled it in his arms like a newborn baby.

His bare feet whispered across the carpet as he quietly walked to the foot of the bed he shared with his wife. Closing his eyes, George took a deep breath and let it out slowly. After a few seconds, his eyelids fluttered open, his lips pressed together, and his brows drew down as he focused on what must be done. Sliding the stock back and forth, he chambered a shell, the sound shattering the silence and startling Jen awake.

For a brief moment, as her eyes shot open, she didn't see her husband. When she finally did catch a glimpse of him, she thought she was in the throes of a nightmare. "This isn't real," she insisted, her whispered voice cracking. A second later, Jen realized that nothing could be further from the truth.

Like a scene straight out of the *Amityville Horror*, George squeezed the trigger. The shotgun blast was deafening in the enclosed space, making everything sound as if it were underwater, and the quick burst of fire that licked from the end of the barrel blinded him for a moment.

"Why?" Jen's eyes pleaded with him as the life rushed out of her body and blood began to saturate the sheets and blankets.

Not deigning to dignify her dying question with an answer, George turned and walked out into the hallway. Focused on his next target, he didn't notice the glowing, yellow eyes watching on from the darkened corner of the hall. As he chambered a second shell, Cassie stepped out of her room. "Daddy? Is that you?" Her voice trembled and she cried; it took every ounce of courage she had to not run back into her room and hide under her bed.

Before George could pull the trigger again, Cassie saw the yellow glow of the monster's eyes behind her father. Her screams only lasted for a fraction of a second, though. The shotgun roared to life once more, sending chunks of bloody flesh and bone against the wall behind Cassie, leaving only a mangled flap of mutilated skin where her head and neck had once been. Her tiny body twitched for nearly half a minute, as if it didn't realize the girl was dead, then fell to the floor.

"That was beautiful," the Black Knight hissed with glee, clapping his bony hands together. "Now, it's time to move on to bigger and better things."

Chapter 14

As the platform neared the bottom of the hill, its three riders braced themselves for the sharp bend in the tracks ahead. Katie had a brief flash of a roller coaster she had ridden at Cedar Point ages ago. Once, when she had rode the Demon Drop with her friends, they had told her about a neat trick. "If you put a penny in the palm of your open hand as the ride plummets you to the bottom, the coin will float in the air." The words of her friend forced her to recall the time she had attempted the very same trick. The one thing her friend didn't warn her about, though, was that you needed to be careful at the end of the ride when the car quickly sloped from its vertical descent and rolled up the tracks horizontally as the brakes were applied. The result of the omission had given her a considerable welt on her forehead. When the momentum of the ride changed, the hovering coin had smacked her in the head right between the eyes.

Raising a hand to rub the spot above her brow where the penny had struck her years ago, she was nearly thrown from the rail-car as it careened around the sharp turn. It seemed like the mother of all miracles that none of them had been ejected from the platform as the braking system engaged. The metal wheels screeched their protest and sparks showered from the rails as the car slowly ground to a stop.

Breathing a sigh of relief that none of them had been injured over the course of their brief, downhill ride, Katie jumped off the platform and helped Brian and Julie to the ground. During their descent, the rush of adrenaline coursing through their bodies had caused them to temporarily forget about the chill of the night air around them, but now that the boost of endorphins was beginning to wear off they were quickly reminded of this fact. Shivering, goosebumps dotting the landscape of her bare flesh as if she had just entered puberty and was covered with acne, Julie wrapped her arms tightly around her midsection.

With the urgency of their rapid departure behind them, Brian finally had a moment to gather his thoughts. As he began to relax, Julie's nakedness registered in his mind and he quickly averted his eyes. After a few seconds passed, the touch of a hand on his arm startled him. Hesitantly, he turned his head slightly. "Oh, it's you." His relieved breath rushed from his lungs when he saw Katie standing beside him.

"If it's not too much to ask, can I borrow your shirt for a little while? At least until we can find appropriate clothing for Julie?"

"Of course. I don't know why I didn't think of that," he replied, hastily shedding his top and handing it to Katie.

"Thanks!" She managed to suppress her laughter, but not her grin. Even in the moonlight, which filtered through the trees at the edge of the tracks, Katie could tell the man was blushing. She couldn't help but think how uncommon such a chivalrous act was back on Earth. That wasn't her experience since coming to Desolace, though. Here, that type of thing seemed almost commonplace.

With chattering teeth, Julie thanked Katie for the shirt and slipped it on. Since she was a few inches shorter than Brian, the top hung slightly lower on her body, but not low enough to cover the tufts of her pubic hair. "I don't suppose you have anything to cover my bottom half, do you?" The pleading look in her eyes echoed the question louder than the soft rasp of her voice, which was barely audible and sounded as if she had been gargling gravel or smoking cigarettes for about seventy years.

"Let me check our supplies." Dropping a hand to her side, Katie fumbled for the bag she had taken with her when she and Brian had left town this morning. Frantically, she patted her hand around her belt line, thinking the supplies had shifted on their journey. It was gone! "Shit! Hang on a sec, Julie," she said, her raised voice startling Brian.

His feet shuffled across the loose dirt beside the tracks as he strode toward them. "What's wrong?"

"I lost our bag of supplies," Katie admitted glumly. "Help me look for it. Maybe it flew over the side of the platform when we rounded that last corner." She tried to remain hopeful, but the more she thought about it the less likely it seemed they would find the object. *I'm not even sure I had it with me when we fled the room where we found Julie.*

After canvassing the area near the bend in the tracks for nearly half an hour, Brian raised both of his palms to the sky as he shrugged his shoulders. "Maybe it fell from the car as we were coming down the hill," he suggested.

"I hope so, Brian. I would hate to think that I somehow managed to forget it at the top," she stated, exhaling sharply in exasperation, silently cursing herself for not paying attention.

"What's done is done. I think it's time we go check on Edward." His lips pursed together in a tight-lipped smile that looked more like a grimace.

"Who?" Julie glanced at her best friend nervously.

Gently, Katie grasped Julie's hand and urged her forward. "He's a great guy, who also happens to be a wizard."

Agitated that Amber had thwarted his plans for the hapless sorcerer, George angrily stalked back and forth between two buildings on the outskirts of the abandoned town as he considered a way to coax the woman's spirit away from the human she guarded. As he continued pacing, the steady *clack ... thump, clack ... thump,* of metal on metal broke through the veil of silence that had lain over the town like a shroud.

The first thought which came to him was that the demons were returning to finish what they'd started, riding the flatbed train car as if it were a giant surfboard. It would be less work for him if that were the case, but George also remembered the Black Knight's sneaky plot to have the creatures get rid of him. Drifting to the back side of the structure beside him, the one which faced the mountain, he quickly floated toward the inn.

When he arrived a few moments later, George glanced around in search of a hiding place. Within seconds he found the perfect camouflage. A shaft of moonlight shimmered off of the pile of corpses stacked against the rear wall of the inn. The illumination would disguise the presence of his glowing form well enough to mask him from anyone who casually glanced in his direction. Quickly, he slipped behind the wall of dead bodies and defunct cyborgs, crouching low to remain unseen and still allow him to view the area surrounding the tracks.

Looking on with great anticipation, George caught a quick glimpse of the rail-car as it sped around the bend at the bottom of the hill. Immediately afterward, he heard a loud, screeching noise as someone applied the brakes. Tiny showers of sparks were visible through the foliage until the platform came to a stop. Tensely, he watched, waiting for the surge of demons to appear.

After what seemed like an eternity, his excitement grew. It wasn't a horde of foul creatures that strode into view, but three humans. It was difficult to tell from this distance, but one of them looked very familiar. As he continued to study the small group, George realized why. Though the blonde woman appeared to be emaciated beyond what any normal human could survive, the sight of her jarred his memory. *It's that skinny blonde bitch that used to ride my bus! When I gave her to the supervisor at The Factory, I assumed I would never see her face again.* Once George realized who she was, he turned his attention to the dark haired woman beside her. *I know her, too!* If he would have had hands to rub together, they would have been doing so now, vigorously. It felt almost as if the Black Knight had dropped the two girls in his lap as a gift. *Playtime is coming soon, my dears.* A wicked grin suffused his misty features as he contemplated the return to his former glory.

Before entering the inn to check on Edward, Katie veered over toward the mechanical horses. At first, Julie didn't realize what the darkened shapes were that they approached, but as the moon above them crept from behind a cloud her eyes grew wide in panic, vaguely recalling a hazy memory of the metal creatures. She shook her head violently, digging her feet into the dusty ground as she attempted to backpedal and pull Katie away from the monstrosities.

Jerked off balance, Katie spun to face her and saw the sheer terror in her eyes. "Relax, Julie," she whispered, briefly recalling the first time she had encountered the beasts and how it had made her feel. "They won't harm you." Again, Katie tugged gently on her friend's hand, but even in her weakened condition Julie didn't budge. Even though she wore nothing except the shirt from Brian's back, Julie began to sweat.

How am I going to convince her that the horses aren't a threat to her? She rolled the question around in her mind for a few seconds when suddenly the solution presented itself. Since Julie's palms were slick with perspiration, Katie attempted to withdraw her hand. "Let go," Katie scolded in a harsh whisper when she failed to slip her friend's clammy grasp. Julie shook her head again in vehement refusal.

Well, plan A didn't work. Now, I need to come up

with a plan B. It was a good thing that she could normally think fast when situations like this arose. Glancing toward the inn, she saw the shirtless shaman waiting impatiently by the door. "Hey, Brian. I need a favor," she called out softly, beckoning him toward her with her broken hand.

Walking over, he stopped beside Katie and bent an expectant ear to her lips. She whispered her plan to him as quietly as she could, hoping that Julie couldn't hear what was being said. When Katie was finished, Brian nodded his head and straightened. With a quick glance toward the frightened woman, he spun on his heel and approached the nearest horse.

A cracked scream erupted from Julie's throat and her eyes bulged from their sockets, her jaw dropping in disbelief. "What are you doing? Get away from it … please! Those things are evil!"

Within arms' reach of the creature, Brian stopped. Turning his head to face Julie, his lips turned upward in a smile as he extended his arm and placed a hand on the mechanical steed. When nothing happened, Julie's expression changed; lines appeared on her forehead, her eyebrows furrowed, and her mouth hung open. She couldn't explain why, but she had been sure the creature would attack. "See, there is nothing to fear," Brian remarked, patting the metal horse to emphasize his point.

Gently, Katie tried again, lightly pulling her friend toward her. "It's okay." She smiled, continuing to coax Julie along.

Even after witnessing what Brian had done, Julie was not entirely convinced that the creature was safe to approach. She dragged her feet in the dirt to slow her progress, but continued moving forward. *Maybe if I take my time it will reveal its true nature.* Sweat seemed to gush from her pores as the distance between them grew shorter and shorter. Still, nothing happened to confirm her fears. *Or, maybe by walking slowly I am keeping it from noticing my presence and getting spooked.* It was a crazy thought, but suddenly she was determined to test her hypothesis. Without warning, Julie released Katie's hand and darted, if that was what you called her accelerated, gimpy gate, toward the metallic creature.

"What the ..." Katie gasped in shock as her friend rushed by.

The only reaction from the beast was the silent swivel of one head. A lone red glow regarded Julie with indifference. She tried to brace herself for impact, but her limbs weren't working the way they should have. With her arms only halfway raised, she slammed into the side of the mechanical steed and her feet flew out from beneath her, causing a small dust cloud as she landed hard on her butt. The creature didn't budge, and though she found it hard to believe, made no move to attack any of them.

"What was all that about?" Brian laughed, bending down to offer his hand to Julie. As Katie joined them, she let out a soft, exasperated sigh and shrugged her shoulders.

Once on her feet again, Julie brushed herself off and hung her head. She didn't know why she felt ashamed, especially considering the horrors she had endured during her time on Desolace, but somehow she did. She should have believed Katie when she'd told her the machines were harmless.

When she didn't reply, Brian put a finger under her chin and gently raised her head to face him. Streaks of tears blazed crooked paths down her dirty cheeks. Not sure what had prompted them, he did the only thing he could think of. "It's okay. Everything will be all right," he remarked in a soothing tone, wrapping his arms lightly around her in a comforting hug.

Behind them, Katie rummaged through the one remaining saddle bag after removing it from behind the saddle. Pulling the only useful item she could find from it, she approached Julie and tapped lightly on her shoulder. Her face was buried in Brian's scrawny chest, but she turned her head toward Katie.

With a weak smile, Katie held up a ragged piece of cloth, which was a remnant of their time on future Earth. Separating herself from Brian's embrace, she regarded Katie with a puzzled expression. "What's that for?"

Though Julie's voice was a barely audible croak, she understood perfectly. "I'll show you." She smiled. Bending down, Katie wrapped the strip of cloth around her friend's waist and knotted the ends together on her hip. Standing up, she took a step back to admire her handiwork and grinned. "Voila! Now you have a skirt to match your fashionable top," Katie announced dramatically. For the first time since their departure from Cemetery Hill, Julie's face lit up with a smile.

"I don't suppose there was another shirt in that bag, was there?" Brian raised an eyebrow questioningly.

"No such luck. Maybe we can find something to replace it after we rejoin Edward in the inn," Katie suggested. "If not, perhaps Jack will loan you some of his fur."

"Ha, ha. Very funny," he commented sarcastically, shivering as the night breeze picked up slightly.

Turning her eyes on the darkened building, Katie wondered how Edward had fared in their absence. She had almost expected to see light coming from one or more of the windows, but there was none. Suddenly, it felt as if there was a rock sitting in her stomach, as if her guts were trying to tell her that there was something drastically wrong. Driven by her intuition, Katie launched into a sprint, dreading what she would find when she burst through the door.

Confused, Brian froze in place as he watched Katie dart toward the structure, wondering what had suddenly lit a fire in her. He cringed as she flung herself into the door, slamming it open with her body and nearly knocking it from its hinges. In a matter of seconds, screams pierced the night air.

Katie blasted through the doorway and her feet skidded out from beneath her on the slippery floor. As a result, she tumbled through the air for a moment, every limb flailing the air in search of something to break her fall. For a split second she caught a glimpse of something on the floorboards in front of her. Though its shape told her that it was human, the instant before she crashed on top of it Katie realized it wasn't moving to get out of her way. With a bone crunching thud she landed on the object, which turned out to be a block of ice. Broken shards skittered across the floor in every direction as her weight pulverized the frozen form, reminding her of when Edward had turned the invading zombies pouring from Outpost 13 into blocks of ice. Blocks that Jack had immediately destroyed with his powerful claws. As she sat up and shook off the force of her fall, an agonized scream resounded from nearby.

"Nooooooo! Mother!" From the veil of the protective bubble he'd hidden inside of, Edward emerged.

Chapter 15

As he patiently waited for his opportunity, George watched the trio walk toward him then disappear around the side of the building. For a few seconds, he considered following them. Especially after discovering who the two girls were, the students from his bus that would have blown the whistle on his activities had he not taken matters into his own hands. The desire for revenge swirled like a storm cloud in his mind. The feeling was so overwhelming that it nearly blotted out all other thoughts, but deep inside he knew if he rushed blindly ahead to quench his fury, something terrible would happen. As difficult as it was, he had to restrain himself. There would be plenty of other chances to sate his vengeance. It was just a matter of time.

A scream from within the structure brought him out of the vortex of his thoughts. He wasn't positive, but it had sounded like the wizard. There were a few possibilities that suggested themselves to George regarding Edward's outburst, and each one brought a huge grin to his misty features.

Feeling it would be best to keep his distance from the small group—at least for a while, long enough for them to grow confident in his absence—George turned his attention toward the platform resting on the railroad tracks, wondering if there were more potential victims for him to toy with where the rail-car had come from.

Startled by the sudden scream, Katie scrambled backward, sending shards of the frozen woman skittering across the floorboards. As she attempted to flee the potential threat, Edward stepped from the darkness as if a magician had waved a wand and caused him to reappear. The look on his tormented face gave him the appearance of someone who had gone insane. Katie wasn't entirely sure how to react, especially since it seemed like he was looking right through her instead of at her; almost as if his mind couldn't comprehend that she was really in front of him, like she was an illusion or a hallucination. Behind her, the door flew open again.

"What's going—" Brian's question died in his throat. As moonlight framed his and Julie's bodies in the open doorway, he gazed in horror at the carnage before him. A coppery scent hung in the air, reminding him of the stench he associated with slaughterhouses, causing his stomach to lurch. If he had been there moments before, when Katie had accidentally crushed the icy form of Edward's mother, he would have likely been vomiting uncontrollably.

Falling to his knees, Edward scooped up one of the ice chunks, one that contained what remained of Victoria's face, it's features frozen in agonized terror. Ignoring the others, he stroked her rigid, icicle-like strands of hair. Tears streamed down his cheeks as he wailed with grief. "Why couldn't you have stayed home in Elysia?"

As Edward continued to sob, Katie slowly crawled toward him. When she was beside him, she gently placed an arm on his shoulder. Feeling his body trembling beneath her touch as she hugged him, he still seemed to be unaware of her presence. Glancing toward Brian and Julie, she wondered if there was anything at all that would comfort Edward. Katie didn't want to think about letting his grief run its course. It could be days, maybe even weeks, before that would happen and she knew they didn't have time for it. A flash of the forgotten bag in Cemetery Hill floated through her mind, a grim reminder of just how little time they had. They needed to get their wits about them and get the hell out of this town before something came down the hill after them. It was at that moment when Katie realized something else was off.

"Where's Jack," she inquired softly, using the fingers of her broken hand to gently force Edward to look at her. She had thought that pulling his gaze from the fragment of Victoria's shattered face would have lessened his grief and allowed him to regain his focus, but instead he appeared to sink into a deeper depression. The pained look on his face was almost too much to bear.

His breath hitched and tears cascaded from his cheeks like a waterfall. "Jack … is … dead," he barely managed to choke out before his sobs took over again.

Katie and Brian both inhaled sharply at the same time, the revelation catching them completely off guard.

"Wh-what? H-how?" she stammered, her eyes growing moist, her breath seemingly stuck in her throat, as if she'd just been sucker punched.

"I … I don't know." Edward's voice cracked as he

hung his head. It shamed him that he had allowed a spirit to get the better of him, but he knew that the others deserved to hear the truth. Attempting to gather himself, he wiped at his eyes with the back of his hand and let out a hitching breath through his pursed lips. "I think the ghost that Amber tried to warn us about …" He paused, a grimace of pain crossing his features. "I think it got inside of me, took over my body somehow."

Brian glanced around the room nervously, trying to sense if the evil spirit was still present, or possibly even residing inside of Edward and attempting to trick them. After a moment's consideration, he dismissed the idea. *If either of those thoughts were accurate, I would be having trouble breathing. Obviously, the spirit did what it came for and left.* Though he didn't find evidence of the spirit in the dim interior of the inn, Brian saw a pile of scattered limbs not far from where Edward was and couldn't help but wonder if they were Jack's remains.

Katie's jaw dropped open, as if she was dumbfounded and unable to comprehend what Edward had told her. At the very least, she found it difficult to believe that someone with his powers could be susceptible to spiritual persuasion, let alone actually being possessed by one.

Seeing the look in her eyes, Edward knew she didn't believe what he was telling her. Grudgingly, he set the shard of his mother's countenance aside. Shrugging her arm from his shoulder, he scooted away from her slightly and pointed to the area a few feet behind where he'd been sitting.

Throwing a hand over her open mouth to stifle the

shocked gasp bubbling up from her throat, Katie looked at the small pile of body parts in disbelief. She shut her eyes for a moment, desperately hoping what she'd seen was either a mirage or a dream. Tears began to leak from her tightly closed eyelids. Somehow, she knew the carnage would still be there when she opened them, so she turned her head away.

Though the grief of losing his mother and a good friend, in the same day, weighed heavily on his mind, Edward inched closer to Katie and did what he could to console her. As he did, Edward noticed that there was only one person standing in the open doorway. There had been two a minute ago, he could swear to it! He opened his mouth to say something, but nothing came out. Instead, he pointed toward the vacated spot beside Brian.

Following the line of his finger, the shaman spun around, thinking Edward was trying to warn him of danger. At first he didn't notice anything out of place, but as he turned back to face the wizard he caught a glimpse of Julie. Apparently the sight of the carnage inside had been too much for her fragile mind. She was curled up in a near fetal position with her back resting against the outer wall of the inn. "Perhaps you should come outside," Brian suggested, turning back to face Edward.

With a questioning rise of one eyebrow, Edward rose to his feet with a little help from Katie. Carefully stepping around the scattered slivers of ice and sticky splotches of blood, he joined the shaman in the doorway with Katie following on his heels. "Are you sensing something? Has the spirit returned?" He met the gaze of Brian's light blue eyes, which shimmered in the moonlight like silver coins.

"No. I think the sights and smells inside were too much for her," he replied, nodding his head toward the woman, curled into a tight ball against the exterior wall of the inn.

"Who is she, and where did you find her?"

Poking her head past Edward, Katie glanced to see what they were discussing. "That's my friend, Julie. Remember, she is the person you were going to help me find."

At the mention of her name, Julie looked up. Immediately, Edward saw the similarities between the frail, anorexic woman before him and the machine which appeared to be her that they had traveled with in the past. Turning toward Katie, he bent down and whispered in her ear, "Are you positive that it's her this time? Not another machine sent to trick us?"

"Absolutely," she nodded, "we found her near the top of the hill, inside of some sort of torture chamber. It took a bit of effort, but we freed her and brought her with us." Thoughts of the others, still held captive in the crucifix filled room, crossed her mind. She wished there was a way to free them all, but Katie knew it would be too time consuming. Who knew when something, or someone, would come through the darkened vortex that had been in the corner. For that matter, it could have already happened. "Shit!"

Edward had started to look back toward the emaciated girl, but Katie's curse snapped his attention back to her. "What?"

She hesitated briefly, biting her lower lip, not wanting to admit her screw-up. "I accidentally left our supply bag up there."

"That's not a big deal. We can acquire more items along the way. Our journey is far from over," Edward stated, managing a thin smile that he hoped would reassure her.

Instead of returning his smile, she hung her head. "It's not the supplies that I'm worried about," Katie mumbled. "There was a portal in the room, and we left in a hurry because we thought someone was getting ready to come through. If we were right, then I'm sure the bag will be discovered. They will almost certainly know that we were there, and that we took something from them."

Sighing, Edward rubbed his face with a far off look in his eyes as he contemplated her revelation. As he was about to reply, Amber suddenly appeared around the corner of the building, interrupting his train of thought. She was pulsating in the same manner as was normally indicative of her being afraid.

"You have to get out of here while you can," she warned. "The evil spirit which has been following you has left and gone up the hill."

"And, this isn't a good thing?" Edward looked more confused than ever. *If the ghost is gone, it should give us a little time to regroup.*

"Nothing he does is good. I've got a very bad feeling about this. For all I know, he could be going to get reinforcements," Amber insisted, her glowing form blinking even more rapidly.

Great! If Amber is right, things could be going from bad to worse really fast! She hadn't thought that her mistake would escalate their problems so quickly, but the one thing she did know was that she didn't want to hang around to find out. Katie glanced from one face to the next, trying to ascertain if the others were feeling the same oppressive dread she felt, tightening like a noose around their necks. From what she could tell, everyone except Edward seemed unsettled by Amber's theory. For whatever reason, the wizard looked more angry and determined. His pale, gray eyes gleamed with what appeared to be an unquenchable hatred, as if the mere thought of their situation had caused an irrevocable snap in his mind. Katie had never seen such a look in his eyes, and seeing it now scared the living shit out of her.

Gently, Brian tapped Katie on the shoulder. "I hate to admit it, but I think Amber is right," he told her as she came out of the haze of her thoughts and turned to face him. He waited for a minute for her to respond, but when she didn't, he motioned with his head for Katie to go into the inn with him. "Help me gather some blankets, and anything else you think we can use."

When Brian mentioned going inside to replenish some of their supplies, Edward recalled with sorrow something which still required his attention before they departed. Stepping over to where Julie cowered against the building, he tilted her chin up. "Will you be all right out here by yourself for a minute or two?" Without a word, she nodded her head. "I'll be back as soon as I can," he promised, then turned and disappeared through the door.

Once he was gone, Julie caught movement in the corner of her eye and shifted her head to the left for a better view. Her jaw dropped to her chest as she saw the flickering ghost a few feet away. At first, she couldn't control the terrified trembling of her body, but as she remained focused something jarred loose in Julie's memory. Something familiar. She couldn't place it yet, but there was … *Holy crap!* Was it possible? Could this be the wretched ghost from what seemed like a lifetime ago? The one that she and Katie had contacted on the Ouija board?

Struggling to her feet, Julie stumbled toward the apparition. As she got closer, the bright and dim pulses of Amber's glow grew less frequent, almost as if the ghost was recalling the same distant memory.

"Do I know you? Something about you seems familiar to me," Amber intoned.

Hearing the spirit's voice, Julie was sure now. This was the same ghost who had led herself and Katie to a house to show them who her killer was. The psychopath that turned out to be their school bus driver, and the man who had abducted Julie and brought her to this awful world. "How … how did you get here?" Even though her voice was raspy and cracked, Amber seemed to understand her perfectly.

"I came here with Katie," she replied. "I was hoping she could help me find my killer and rid the world of his evil, but it seems he is just as vile in death. I've also been trying to help Katie find you. I'm glad at least one of us has gotten what we came here for," Amber added, a slight note of sarcasm in her hollow voice.

Distracted by the sound of the door opening behind her, Julie turned and saw Edward exiting the inn with a large bundle in his arms. Silently, he slipped past the two of them and disappeared around the corner of the building. Before she could inquire about what he was doing, Brian and Katie emerged. Both of their arms were loaded with items they had pilfered from inside, the shaman now sporting a blanket knotted around his neck like a superhero's cape, as they quietly made their way to the mechanical beasts waiting nearby to distribute their bounty on the backs of the creatures. When they finished, the two of them approached Amber and Julie.

"Has Edward come back out yet? We didn't see him inside."

Answering Katie's question, Amber pointed toward the area between the structures.

"Can you check on him please, Brian?" Katie pleaded, feeling like Julie would be more comfortable if she stayed by her side.

With a nod, the shaman vanished into the darkness between the buildings. Less than a minute later he reappeared. "He's laying Jack to rest and asked to be alone until he's finished," Brian told them in a hushed tone.

Chapter 16

When the screams broke out, sounding as if they came from within the inn, it took phenomenal restraint for him to stay where he was. George didn't want to risk being seen because he was being impulsive. There would be plenty of other opportunities to witness the torment of the small group, which would be easier during daylight hours when his glowing form wasn't visible. If he could manage to whittle their numbers down to one or two, masking his presence wouldn't matter as much.

As he considered his next move, a roar unlike anything George had ever heard drowned out the agonized wails of the nearby humans. It seemed to emanate from the mountain before him, but it was impossible to tell for sure without investigating. The angry outburst carried the punch of an enormous pride of mountain lions, all roaring at the same moment, but as the intensity of the sound began to diminish, George got the impression that the noise was not made by animals. At least, not any he had ever seen up close.

After waiting for a couple of minutes to see if the sound would repeat itself, which it did not, his curiosity began to surface. Deciding that he needed a distraction to keep him busy until daylight, George drifted away from the building and floated uphill.

Dragging the younger version of George into the woods across the street from his home, the Black Knight pulled him through the black void of the portal. As the two of them stepped into Cemetery Hill, the vortex swirled for a second before collapsing in on itself.

The sensation of being ripped apart, and put back together again, reminded George of the pod-like mechanisms that ultimately created a being known as the *Brundlefly* in one of his favorite movies. Blinking his eyes rapidly, he tried to focus on the sight before him in the deep red gloom of the chamber he now stood in. As his vision adjusted to the dimness, the spectacle in front of him took his breath away. "What the …" Row upon row of tall, wooden crucifixes greeted his confused mind, the sight reminiscent of something straight out of a *Dracula* movie; a scene which depicted hundreds or thousands of people, skewered atop long, wooden spikes by *Vlad the Impaler*. Although, the smattering of people upon the crosses were not impaled by any means. Instead, they were held in place by chains and metal bands, which brought the memory of the torture chamber he had constructed in his own basement to the forefront of his mind.

Breaking George from his confused thoughts, the Black Knight suddenly let out an ear shattering roar. Clapping his hands over his ears in an attempt to muffle the sound, he squinted toward the entity who now stood beside an empty crucifix. When the deafening roar subsided, George cautiously approached the cloaked figure.

Carefully choosing his words, he addressed the demon in a tone he hoped would not antagonize him. "I must admit, this place was a lot to take in at first," George remarked, trying to sound as casual as he could. "I hope you don't think that I'm ignorant for asking, but I can't help wondering what has angered you?"

Spinning around with inhuman speed, the Black Knight bent down slightly, his hideous face so close to George's that he could see the saliva dripping from the demon's fangs and taste the creature's foul breath as it washed over him. "This is what bothers me," the Black Knight hissed, dangling the strap of a bag from one, skeletal finger. "Someone has dared to enter my chamber and take something from me. When I find out who, I am going to string them up in here for the rest of their miserable, pathetic lives. There will be no end to the suffering I will unleash upon them," he growled.

Raising his hands in a submissive gesture, George backed up and put a couple of paces between them. "Sorry I asked. Just remember, I'm on your side."

"It better stay that way, too, George," the Black Knight stated, his voice dripping with malice.

Unsure of what he would find, though he suspected it would be a large assemblage of the tiny, impish demons, George followed the railroad tracks. Thankful that he hadn't been forced to climb the mountain as a human, he quickly ascended the hill. As he came to the final bend in the tracks, he saw a darkened shape, like the mouth of a cave, nearby.

Initially, when he floated through the opening, George was impressed with the setup of the expansive chamber that had been hidden from sight until he had entered. Mesmerized by the blood red illumination of the interior, he drew closer. Admiring the intricate layout—cross-like pillars spaced evenly throughout what he had originally thought to be a cave—of a torture chamber worthy of his wildest dreams, memories of his former life flashed through his mind. When he saw that many of these constructs were bearing nude, human bodies, he drifted carelessly about, inspecting the prisoners. He didn't realize that he wasn't alone until he heard a seething voice utter his name. Whipping around toward the sound, the first thing George saw was a tall, cloaked figure with its back turned. The voice should have been immediately familiar, especially considering how many times it had spoken directly to him in the past, but instead it only instilled a sense of déjà vu in his mind.

Suddenly, another face appeared. It had been hidden from view, until now, by the towering frame of the Black Knight, but as his shocked mind attempted to comprehend what he was seeing, his eyes insisted that he was gazing into a mirror. The man, partially shielded from view, was a spitting image of himself. Albeit, a younger version. George watched as the man caught a glimpse of his ghostly form, the younger version's eyes widening in surprise.

The younger man rose a shaky finger and pointed in his direction. Barely managing to slip behind the upright of the nearest crucifix before the Black Knight turned his attention toward him, George waited for the inevitable.

Even though nothing happened at first, he kept himself hidden.

"What?" the Black Knight growled impatiently as his glowing, yellow eyes followed the man's unsteady finger. "Why are you shaking like a coward? I hope you aren't going to be as useless as my last protégé. I have better things to do than be your fucking nursemaid."

"There ... I saw something over there," he stated, his trembling legs already beginning to carry him toward the nearly transparent form he'd seen just moments before. Hesitantly, he stopped in front of the empty cross that he was certain a ghostly form was on the other side of. He could feel the penetrating leer of the Black Knight, searing through his flesh like a branding iron. After a few seconds, he assumed the cloaked figure had turned the burning embers of his eyes elsewhere because the sensation was suddenly gone. Gathering his resolve, he dared a peek behind the pillar. A shocked gasp escaped his lips as he felt something invade his body.

After surveying the rest of the large room and finding no other prisoners missing, the Black Knight turned his attention back to George. "I have to leave this place for a while so I can take care of some business. I need you to stand guard here until I return. Do you think you can handle that?"

Though the spirit had successfully invaded young George's body, it receded from the man's mind and faded into the background, fearing that if he remained in firm possession of the fleshy shell that the Black Knight would almost certainly sense it. "I ... I think so," he replied nervously.

"Good. Take up a position just outside. There should be plenty of places you can remain out of sight. If anyone dares to approach, kill them." Not waiting to see if George would ask more questions, or complain about what was being asked of him, the Black Knight swiftly turned and exited the chamber.

Even with the departure of the cloaked figure, George only managed to relax slightly. The demon hadn't stated it out loud, but he had heard the underlying malice in the Black Knight's voice; the veiled threat of indescribable torture should he fail in his duties.

Before heading outside, he perused the chamber in search of a weapon he could use if a situation arose that required it, stopping for a few seconds here and there to appraise naked prisoners. The vast majority were repulsive to gaze upon. They might have been attractive to him at one point in their lives, but many of them looked extremely malnourished, emaciated to the degree that they reminded him of those fucked up commercials he used to see from time to time. The ones which displayed one skeletal Ethiopian child after another, trying to pull on the heartstrings of the viewer and get them to send a donation, claiming the small price would help feed the kid for a month. Somehow, George didn't think any of that money ever made it across the world to where it was supposed to go, but disgustedly regarded the pleas as a scam intended to line the pockets of some shady businessman somewhere.

Glancing up at the scant form of what he thought was a woman—her skin clinging so tightly to her bones that her ribs and pelvis threatened to burst through the thin layer of her flesh—he couldn't help but wonder how long she had been held captive, or how she was being kept alive. Forcing himself to study her body more closely, George discovered puncture marks in areas that still had a semblance of meat on the bones. *They must be feeding her with an IV or something. Giving her just enough nourishment to sustain life. It would certainly explain the lack of excrement, which should have been stinking up the place to high heaven.* Although George enjoyed torturing and killing people, this place sickened him. It would be the greatest mercy of all to give these poor souls the release of death.

Unable to look at the woman any longer, he dropped his eyes to the floor and shuffled away, heading toward the outside exit. As he walked, George felt a twinge within his body. At first he didn't recognize it for what it truly was, dismissing it as one of the rare emotions that tried to bubble to the surface of his mind, but then the belief was shattered as he realized what was happening. A fleeting thought traveled through his brain; the temporarily forgotten memory of the ghost he had seen a short while ago. *I'm being possessed!* As if to confirm this, a familiar voice echoed in his head. "Hello, me … It's me, again."

Chapter 17

Although Katie and Brian had expressed their opinions to Edward regarding the urgency of their departure from the town nestled at the base of the mountain, nothing they said swayed him from his duties as a friend and as the leader of their small entourage. He insisted on honoring Jack with a proper burial, though the only way he could accomplish this task was to cover his friend's mutilated appendages with rocks, as well as paying his respects. During this time, Edward lit a small campfire near the grave site, compelling them to reminisce and tell stories of their fondest memories of their fallen comrade. Many of these tales brought tears to Katie's eyes, dredging up painful recollections of the other friend they had lost along the way, Mike.

Brian hadn't known Jack as long as the others, and had never met Mike, but it didn't slow the flow of liquid that trickled down his cheeks. Even Julie seemed sadder than expected. She didn't know any of them, other than Katie, and even though she was wary of them, Julie felt like she could trust them. After all, they were Katie's companions. If her best friend in the world could place her faith in these strangers, then shouldn't she do the same? *God, I hope I never have to do something like this for Katie,* she thought. *Or her for me.*

By the time everyone had finished paying homage to

Jack, the first light of dawn was beginning to creep onto the horizon. One by one they wiped the moisture from their eyes and stood, dreading the thought of leaving another companion behind. Each individual pulled their pilfered blanket tightly around their body to stave off the early morning chill in the air as they stepped away from the fire, looking as if they wore the shrouds of vagrants. They tried to keep their minds occupied with thoughts of things to come, instead of dwelling on their past mistakes and losses, carefully making certain that they had everything packed for the coming journey. Despite his best efforts, Edward looked wistfully toward the inn, wishing he could afford his mother a proper burial but knowing that collecting the frozen fragments of her body would be like finding needles in a haystack. It was almost certain he would never find them all, and burying part of her seemed like sacrilege, as if by doing so would somehow make her soul incomplete.

Taking a few minutes before leaving, Edward rifled through the remaining saddlebag and distributed some dried meat and fruit to everyone, citing the fact that the journey ahead would be a long one and they would need every ounce of energy the food could provide. It was something he deemed especially important for Julie, who appeared to be on the verge of skeletal from the abuse she had endured during her captivity.

Once they were satisfied that all was in order and they could get underway, another unforeseen problem reared its ugly head. Though Brian had shown Julie that the two mechanical horses were not a threat to her wellbeing, she shook her head and shied away when it was time to go and everyone was starting to mount up. Edward glanced at Katie from his position behind the shaman on one of the beasts. The pleading look in his gaze spoke to her without having to utter a single word. *Please, do whatever you must to convince her. Time is short, and we have to get underway.*

Julie was trembling when Katie stopped in front of her, putting a hand lightly on each shoulder and dropping her head slightly to meet her friend's terrified eyes. "You know I would never ask you to do anything that would hurt you, right?"

"It's not you that I worry about," she replied, her voice still scratchy from disuse. "I know what these … things … are designed to do, and what they are capable of."

"What do you mean?" Katie lifted one eyebrow in pained confusion.

"Do you remember a while back? When I told you I was being held in a place called the Factory?"

"Yes. What about it?"

"While I was there, before they sent me to the awful place you rescued me from, I was forced to build a couple of those things," she croaked, pointing disgustedly at the mechanical beast.

"They're only a means of transportation, right?" The puzzled look on Katie's face caused deep, wrinkled lines to appear on her forehead.

"Yes, and no." Julie shook her head sadly. "They are meant for much more than that. There is a hollow area in their chests, accessed by a locking plate, which has numerous implications. The area inside is large enough to hold probably two or three human beings, maybe four if they are packed in like sardines."

"Hold that thought," she told Julie, raising a finger and turning to face Edward. "Did you know those things have a hidden compartment?" The look of shock on his face told her everything she needed to know. He had no idea! Suddenly, a terrible thought came to her. *What if the evil bastard, who forced Julie into servitude, is hiding something in the bellies of the very beasts we're riding? If that's the case, he could be sitting around just waiting for an opportunity to catch us off guard!*

While Edward sat behind Brian, slack-jawed, as if he couldn't begin to fathom her question, Katie strode to the beast she intended to ride. Squatting down, she searched every fold in the metal for a potential hinge that might tell her where the cavity in the horse's chest was located. Finding a barely noticeable crease on the beast's chest, she ran her fingers down its length, poking and prying the edge in an attempt to pull it open. When every effort was met with failure, she slammed her fist into the metal plate in frustration and began to turn away. As she did, the heavy steel panel almost knocked her off her feet as it noiselessly swung downward.

After escaping being struck by the chest piece by mere inches, Katie held her breath, almost as if she expected something to emerge from the cavity. When nothing happened, she took a tentative peek into the recess and saw that the hollowed out area inside the creature was exactly how Julie had described it. "I wish we would have known about this when we were shivering and freezing our asses off, trying to shelter ourselves from the unpredictable storms around here." Glancing from one face to the next, she didn't understand why nobody was checking the creature that Brian and Edward were on top of. Katie could understand Julie being apprehensive, but the others? Were they being lazy? *Maybe they are too chicken shit, thinking there might be a surprise inside their steed,* Katie surmised, taking the initiative and stalking to the front of the other machine.

Not wasting any time, Katie stood to one side to avoid being struck when the chest plate swung open. Striking the first beast had caused her good hand to throb, so instead of making it hurt more she bent down and sent a donkey kick at the machine's chest. It worked perfectly, and was much less painful than using her fist. When she didn't see anything pouring forth from the cavity, Katie peeked inside. It was an identically empty space to the one she revealed in her own horse.

Once she had found that both steeds were not carrying any threats to their wellbeing aboard, Katie lifted each panel and pushed them until she heard them latch securely. Trying to lighten the mood, Brian joked with Katie as she strode toward where Julie stood. "Are you done horsing around?"

Spinning to face the shaman, she saw the sheepish smirk on his face. "Ha, ha. You're just a barrel of laughs, Brian," she remarked with a half grin, waving a hand at him dismissively. A few seconds later, she was standing in front of Julie. Even after showing everyone in the group that there was nothing lurking inside the mechanical beasts, lying in wait to spring out and kill them, Julie still looked nervous and afraid. "I won't let anything happen to you again. I promise that I won't let you out of my sight. I will be with you every step of the way," Katie whispered softly, confident that she could uphold her vow.

Her eyes growing moist, Julie nodded hesitantly after a minute of indecision. She knew in her heart that Katie would do everything in her power to protect her and keep her safe. All she could do was hope that Katie's efforts would be enough. Past experience told her that the dangers of this world could easily turn the tide against them, though. "I will try my best to not freak out," Julie croaked, letting her breath out slowly and trying to muster up enough courage to put a foot into the stirrup and mount the metallic beast.

Chapter 18

Sitting on a large rock, just outside the mountainside entrance to Cemetery Hill, George waited for the Black Knight to return. His duties as a sentry seemed like a waste of time to him. After all, who in their right mind would scale the treacherous incline? The demon obviously thought someone might try, considering one of his prisoners was missing, but George didn't think it was very likely. Apparently, the previous intruders had already acquired what they came for, so why risk life and limb to climb up here again?

A sudden bout of nausea washed over him, the surrounding foliage wavered like a mirage, giving him the light-headed feeling of having a few too many drinks. After a few seconds the feeling subsided, but something in his gut told him that things had not returned to normal. The wooziness had passed, but his body still felt strange. As the reason for this feeling crept into his mind, kind of like an 'ah ha' moment, he lost control of his body. The entity, which claimed to be another version of himself, shoved its way forward and pushed his consciousness to the background. It felt a lot like being gagged and duct taped, held hostage in his own mind.

It felt phenomenal to be back in a body that he could call his own. For what seemed an eternity, he had dealt with being unable to touch, feel, taste, and smell the world around him, but those days were behind him now. Running his fingers lightly over the skin of his arms, George relished the sensation that had eluded him since his death. Twisting and bending, George tested the newly acquired suit of flesh and bone for limitations. When he discovered there were none—it was almost as if he had never died—his lips stretched in an evil grin. He couldn't help but wonder if the fleshy disguise would be enough to fool his former master; maybe even get back into his good graces. Not that George truly cared whether the demon liked him or not, but if he could develop trust between himself and the Black Knight again, it would make revenge a much easier goal to accomplish. Especially, considering how casually George had been cast aside when he didn't follow the entity's orders to the letter. Being tricked into a situation that had brought about his demise wasn't something George was prepared to let go of.

The demonic hiss of the Black Knight's voice startled him from his thoughts. As George turned to face him, he wondered if he'd left himself vulnerable and inadvertently allowed the demon to read his mind. "Has anyone approached in my absence?"

Suddenly, his throat seemed clogged with mucus. "No," he managed after clearing his windpipe.

"Goooood," the Black Knight remarked, rubbing his skeletal hands together. "I have a little surprise for you." Although the demon seemed in much better spirits than he was after finding someone had invaded his lair, the writhing mass of flesh beneath his black cowl made him look like a person that belonged locked away in a mental institution.

Not sure that he wanted to know what his surprise was, George raised an eyebrow. His eyeballs danced nervously in their sockets as he hesitantly glanced into the demon's glowing yellow eyes, searching for any sign that the Black Knight knew he was inside the body before him. Unable to maintain eye contact with the entity, George dropped his head and looked at his feet for a few seconds. Knowing he couldn't keep looking away from the demon without raising suspicion, George lifted his head and tried to sound casual. "What sort of surprise?"

At first, George thought when the Black Knight turned his head and peeked through the entrance of Cemetery Hill that he was making sure they were alone. "Come," he hissed. As George was about to step into the blood red light of the interior, his foot stopped in mid-air. The stomping sound of heavy footfalls reverberated in the chamber. The ground shook as whatever the Black Knight had summoned steadily approached.

A rush of air burst from his lungs as the creature came in to view, and it took every ounce of courage to not flee in terror. The beast which rounded the corner and stopped beside the Black Knight was huge! Three pairs of malevolently glowing red eyes stared at George from three separate, massive, wolf-like heads. Though he tried his best to not show that he was afraid, his body betrayed him and began to tremble. The enormous creature reminded him of *Cerberus*, but in his wildest imaginings he had never expected the hell-hound to be so large. The beast's heads were almost level with the Black Knight's shoulders, which told George that the demon-dog was at least six feet tall ... and that was when it was standing on all fours. If it were to rear up on its hind legs it would tower over him! The devilish creature took another stomping step forward, stalking through the entrance and into the fading moonlight outside. It was at that moment when George realized the creature before him was not a mere animal, but a machine. Light glinted off the beast's metal exterior and nearly blinded him with its brilliance, almost as if someone had reflected a five hundred watt light bulb in a mirror he was gazing into.

Flashing a wicked grin that made the rows of his razor, sharp teeth shimmer in the moonlight, the Black Knight patted the machine affectionately. "I can sense your fear and apprehension, but there is no need for either." Side by side, the demon and the mechanical monstrosity took a few steps away from the entrance to Cemetery Hill, allowing George to see the creature in its entirety. "In the days to come, this beast will be your companion. A means to an end that will help you to carry out your mission."

His features relaxed slightly when George realized the Black Knight hadn't brought the creature here to end his life for a second time, although his brows drew downward in confusion. "What ... mission?" he questioned, clearing his throat once more.

"I am going to have you follow a group of people, but from a distance. I don't want them to be aware that you are following them. You will travel under the cover of darkness at all times, resting during daylight hours and keeping yourself hidden."

George opened his mouth, but abruptly shut it.

Knowing the individuals the demon referred to, he had almost blown his cover. He had forgotten, for a brief moment that had nearly been his undoing, the younger version of himself would have had no knowledge of the people the Black Knight spoke of. "I have a few questions," he managed after recollecting his thoughts.

"Ask away," the Black Knight invited.

"First off, why am I following these people?"

"To gather information." The demon grinned. "Your new friend here is equipped with surveillance cameras which will relay images back to me, letting me know what they are doing, where they are going … things of that nature. Does that answer your question?"

"Yes," George nodded, "however, it raises another." For the moment, the Black Knight seemed patient. The demon tilted his head curiously and motioned with a skeletal hand for him to continue. "If this mission requires stealth, then how am I supposed to stay hidden when this thing," George dramatically hiked a thumb at the machine, "is stomping around and giving away our position?"

Throwing back his head, cackling laughter erupted from the Black Knight's grinning mouth. The demon's mirth stretched out for nearly a minute before he answered George, "If you stick to traveling at night like I've instructed, none will hear a sound," the Black Knight chuckled, as if the mortal had told him the funniest joke he'd ever heard.

"I don't see how. Someone would have to be deaf to not hear that thing, and it doesn't take into account the way the ground shakes when it walks, either."

"You worry too much, George." The demon sighed, shaking his head.

"And another thing … how am I supposed to control it? Does it follow me around as if it's my faithful dog? Or does it have a leash?"

The Black Knight howled with laughter again. "Come closer. I will show you how to operate your new steed."

"Steed?" Now his curiosity was piqued. The mechanical creature before him didn't even remotely resemble anything that could be ridden, at least, not comfortably. There was no saddle, which meant no stirrups. He scratched his head trying to figure out how he would mount and dismount such a beast.

As George stood beside the machine, the Black Knight grabbed his wrist with a bony hand. Pulling it toward the creature, the demon navigated George's fingertips to the back side of one of the beast's forelegs. His fingers brushed against a raised bump in the metal's surface. When the Black Knight forced him to push against it as if the anomaly were a button of sorts, the multiple-jointed foreleg folded backwards, creating a series of steps.

Doing his best to not make it obvious that he had half a clue how to operate the mechanical creature, George made it appear that he was hesitant to climb on to the beast's back. As he swung his leg over and sat down, he noticed the familiar, joystick-like control protruding from the area where the three necks joined with the massive shoulders of the machine, but he made no move to reach out for it. Instead, George waited for the Black Knight to instruct him on what to do next.

"Do you see the lever jutting up in front of you?"

"Yes," he replied with a nod.

"It is a means to control your direction of travel. When you are on the ground, push or pull the lever in the direction you wish to go. When you are …"

"Whoa! Wait a second!" George interrupted. "Did you say, when I'm on the ground? Are you implying what I think you are?"

"Let me finish," the Black Knight snapped. The frightened grimace blooming on George's face told him he had the man's undivided attention now. Satisfied, the demon continued its instruction, "As I was saying, when you are in the air, the controls will operate differently. Pushing forward will tell the creature to go down, pulling back will cause it to go higher, and pushing the control to one side or the other will tilt its wings in that direction, causing it to execute a turning maneuver. Be careful when you do this. The harder you push the lever to one side, the tighter the turn will be. If you turn too abruptly, you will likely fly from its back and plummet to your death."

Waiting for a few seconds to make sure the Black Knight was done speaking, he nodded his understanding. "One last question, if I may?"

"What now?" Growling, his flaming yellow eyes bored into the mortal as his patience wore thin.

"You stated that the creature has wings, right? Where are they, and how do I activate them?" He tried his best to keep his voice submissive, not wishing to anger the Black Knight any further. At least, not until he had a solid plan for his revenge.

His foul breath hissed through his elongated fangs as he considered the questions, the glow of his eyes narrowing to slits as he thought. After a moment, the Black Knight realized he had not instructed George on this detail. "Look just beyond the lever. There is a rounded, black spot at the base of the center neck. Simply push it down to activate the wings, and depress it again to collapse them." He thought about warning George to move his legs forward when he brought the wings out and put them away, but since he was still irritated with the mortal he decided not to, even though it was possible the man could lose part of his limbs if he wasn't careful.

Chapter 19

Over the last couple of days, their progress had seemed exceedingly slow. In part, this was due to Julie. She was still terrified of the mechanical creatures they rode upon, but gradually her apprehension was beginning to melt away as a small semblance of her sanity started to return. Two major factors contributed to this slow change in her demeanor, the most obvious being her reunion with Katie. No matter what she felt about the others, or their current situation, Julie trusted her best friend implicitly. She knew that whatever happened, Katie would give her life to protect her. Getting real food in her belly helped her outlook as well. For too long, she had dealt with the jab of needles and being fed through tubes.

Though her stomach had difficulties with the various meats, cheeses, and breads at first, sometimes causing violent bouts of nausea, her body quickly adapted. By the second day, she was no longer getting sick when she ingested the food. Instead, she began to crave the sustenance with the enthusiasm of a pregnant woman. When the third day rolled around, her body started to acclimate. For the first time in what seemed to be forever, she was able to evacuate her bladder and bowels normally. Even though the food she took in was far from being seven course meals, more often than not it was just barely enough to stop the rumbling of her stomach, Julie was beginning to gain some of the weight she lost during her captivity. The lackluster, dullness of her grayish skin began to disappear, and the vibrant appearance of health started to blossom on her features.

When the sun reached its highest point in the sky, Edward tapped Brian on the shoulder, indicating for him to stop. "Let's take a short break and get some food in our bellies," he suggested.

Letting the pommel of the saddle go, it snapped upright, causing the machine to skid to a halt. "Sounds like a plan to me." He grinned over his shoulder at Edward, his stomach rumbling its agreement.

Once all four of them had dismounted, Katie began rummaging through the saddle bag. Frowning as she retrieved the remaining food items inside, she passed small portions to everyone. "Well, we need to figure something out if we want to continue eating." She sighed.

"What do you mean?" Brian asked in a muffled voice, around a mouthful of bread.

"We've exhausted our supply of food, that's what I mean," she replied sadly.

"Hmmm," Brian remarked thoughtfully.

"I guess that means we will have to rely on your hunting skills, then," Edward interjected with a grin.

Katie sighed in exasperation. "That's a good plan, in theory, but I don't have any more arrows. I used every one I had in the battle against those tiny demon things, and none of us thought to scour the town before we left to retrieve any of them that might have been left behind."

"They probably wouldn't have been usable anyway," Brian stated. "They would have been tainted with their disgusting, demonic blood. I'm not sure about anyone else, but I wouldn't want to risk that nasty stuff getting into the meat we stick in our mouths."

"You have a point." Edward grimaced, his stomach turning at the mere thought of putting something so vile inside of his body.

"Then, we're screwed. I can't hunt without arrows. Shooting imaginary projectiles from my crossbow isn't going to kill anything," she remarked sarcastically.

Edward tapped his chin thoughtfully with one finger. After a few seconds, he sauntered over to the saddle bag and reached inside. "It may not be the best solution in the world, but perhaps I can create some new arrows for you," he told her, removing a knife from the bag.

After scavenging the surrounding forest for nearly two hours, Brian returned with a small bundle of branches he had hacked from nearby oaks and other hardwood trees with the sword that had once belonged to Jack. Setting the severed limbs at Edward's feet, he joined the others around the small campfire while the wizard began the tedious task of stripping the bark from each stick and whittling them into shape.

Katie watched him intently as he worked, sincerely hoping that Edward could create usable projectiles for her crossbow. When he finished whittling the first arrow, he offered it to her in his outstretched hand. Plucking the bow from the ground beside her, she stood and walked over to collect the potential arrow. Taking it from him, she turned it this way and that, attempting to determine if it was straight enough to work. Satisfied that it was, she slid the shaft into the guide of her weapon. "Shit!"

"What's wrong?" Edward frowned, glancing up at her with dismay.

"It's too long," she replied, turning the arrow backwards and fitting it into the weapon again. With her finger clamped to the shaft, she handed the projectile back to him as she knelt on the ground beside him. "Cut it here, if you can." She scratched the wood with a fingernail to give him a reference point.

Taking it from her, Edward sighed and went back to work. After a couple of minutes, he handed the shortened projectile back to Katie. "Try it now."

When her face lit up, Edward let out the breath he hadn't realized he was holding and smiled. With the biggest grin on her countenance that he had seen in quite some time, she passed the arrow back to him. "It seems perfect. Make another one exactly like this, then I'll test one to see if it fires properly from the crossbow."

The sun was beginning to set on the horizon as they gathered around the campfire, savoring the fresh rabbit meat with juices running down their chins. Katie's initial test of her new arrows had gone much better than expected. The projectiles Edward had made couldn't have flown with more accuracy if they had been created in a factory on Earth. There had been a couple that weren't entirely straight, but even so, each had been fantastically more usable than Katie could have ever hoped for. She still couldn't load the weapon by herself because of her broken hand, but at least she could now hunt again, making her feel tremendously more useful. Maybe she could teach Julie how to use the crossbow. It would certainly alleviate Katie's shortcomings in battle, should the need arise.

"Holy crap! I feel like a stuffed, Thanksgiving turkey." Julie sighed, patting her bulging tummy and smiling. The comment brought chuckles of laughter from everyone. "I never realized how good you were at hunting," she remarked, glancing toward Katie.

"Yep, I'm a regular jack of all trades." Katie laughed. "The only problem is, I'm not a master of any of them."

"You don't give yourself enough credit. I can say, without a doubt in my mind, that if it weren't for you and your skill set, we would be starving right now. Possibly resorting to gnawing on tree bark." The grin on Edward's face literally beamed with pride and admiration.

"I'm sure you would have no trouble getting by without me." Katie blushed. "You could always zap the little, woodland creatures with one of your spells. It would probably work just as well as what I do."

"Absolutely! Heck, in Edward's case, he could flash fry the little buggers and we could skip cooking them altogether." Brian laughed heartily.

Edward shook his head, his cheeks growing red as he lowered his face to hide the smile spreading across it. Though he wasn't normally one to take being made fun of well, he knew they were only trying to lighten the mood. Even when the humor was created at his expense, he couldn't help but be happy. It had been quite some time since those around him had been so light-hearted, and he was thankful for the reprieve from bickering. They all deserved a moment or two of happiness, especially when he considered what might lay ahead. He'd already buried more of his friends and family than he had ever thought he would in this lifetime, and only the Gods knew how many more he would have to do the same for by the time his journey came to an end.

After Katie's impromptu crossbow lesson for Julie's benefit, the men and women split into separate groups. Each took a two hour shift, keeping the small campfire burning while the others slept. Although Edward had been skeptical about dividing the watches by gender, his paranoia of an attack during the women's shift had been unwarranted, thankfully.

When Brian and Edward's watch was over, and one of Desolace's moons had risen, they quietly roused the sleeping women and prepared to head southward once more.

Chapter 20

After receiving the Black Knight's instructions, a short sword, and a small sack of supplies, George watched the demon disappear into the blood red ambiance of Cemetery Hill and vanish from sight. Eager to test the capabilities of his new steed, he located the black button on the center neck of the machine and depressed it. Within a fraction of a second, two enormous metal wings burst forth from their inconspicuous places, which at first glance had looked like metallic fur on the creature's sides, thrusting his legs forward as they extended fully. Silently, George cursed the Black Knight for not warning him of the sharpened appendages. Lifting his feet, he placed them on top of each wing to steady his balance, then bent to check his calves where the metal edges had struck. A trickle of blood flowed from the back of each leg, but it could have been much worse. Remembering something he'd heard at several times during his life, something about cold slowing the flow of blood from a wound, George pulled back on the lever in front of him. Lightly at first, but when it seemed his steed was sure to collide with tree tops in a matter of seconds, he exerted more backward pressure on the lever.

The creature complied, soaring higher and higher into the night sky. After a few minutes, he noticed how thin the air had become and he allowed the joystick-like control to snap back to its original, upright position, immediately leveling off his ascent. Though the altitude was enough to make catching his breath a difficult task, George couldn't help feeling like some sort of medieval warrior upon a mythical beast, riding into battle. His long, brown locks whipped behind him as the wind rushed over his face, adding to the effect. Doubting that anyone on the ground could hear him, he threw back his head, howling like a werewolf at the moon, basking in his new-found freedom. First, the uncanny luck of being rejoined with a body he could call his own, then knowing he had fooled the Black Knight by hiding in the flesh of his younger self, and finally this magnificent prize the demon had bestowed upon him. What more could he ask for?

Returning to his throne room, the Black Knight's rage boiled over when he saw Verin. "How dare you! I leave to take care of business, only to come back and find you sitting in my chair like you own the place," he growled, his glowing yellow eyes suddenly turning to obsidian.

The formless demon spun around at the sound of his master's voice, retreating from the throne until the bank of monitors prevented him from putting further distance between them. "I ... I was just trying to make sure things ran smoothly until you returned, my Lord," Verin stammered.

"Well, you failed miserably, you worm," the Black Knight spat. "While I was away, and you were supposedly taking care of things, someone entered

Cemetery Hill and stole something from me!"

"Wh—what? I—I didn't see anything on the monitors," he stuttered, trying to shrink away from his master as the demon stalked toward him.

"Then, where did this come from?" The Black Knight held the bag out before him with a long, bony finger. The silence was deafening as he searched Verin's shapeless form, waiting for an answer that didn't seem forthcoming. Frustrated with the lack of response from his minion, he expelled a long, hissing breath through his teeth.

Watching the golden shimmer as it started to return to his master's eyes, Verin prayed it was a good sign. Knowing he'd let the Black Knight down in a big way, he hoped the demon would give him an opportunity to atone for his mistakes.

"I can smell your fear. Rightly so, I should rip your pathetic soul apart for your incompetence. However, you have shown in the past that you don't hesitate to follow orders, and most of those times you performed your tasks perfectly." As the Black Knight spoke, he could sense the minion's terror beginning to evaporate and his confidence growing. "I'm not one to normally allow indiscretions, like the one you committed in my absence, to go unpunished, but time is of the essence so I will deal with that matter at a later juncture. In the meantime, I am going to offer you a chance to redeem yourself. If you should succeed in the mission I'm about to give you, your incompetence will be dismissed. But, if you fail … I don't think I need to finish that sentence," the Black Knight stated venomously.

"What would you have me do to prove myself to you,

my Lord?" Verin inquired.

"Go to the Factory. The supervisor there will be expecting your arrival. Once you are there, assemble my army and go forth into the outside world to crush the mortals that dared to violate my domain. When you accomplish this task, return to my lair so we can prepare my assault on the Throne of the Gods."

"As you wish, my Lord." Verin bowed, wasting no time and drifting into the tunnels beyond his master's lair.

The main entrance of the Factory was standing open upon his arrival a few hours later. Traversing the short hallway between the underground river and the workroom, Verin was greeted by a stout, older gentleman whose closely cropped black hair was streaked with gray. The formless demon knew from prior visits to the facility that the man before him was the one in charge of operations.

"I've been expecting you," the man stated with a tight-lipped smile. "Your name is Verin, correct?"

"Yes," he replied in a gruff voice, wanting to skip the pleasantries and get on with what he came here to do. "What do you have for me?"

"Follow me, please." The supervisor turned and strode to the opposite side of the large work area, stopping before a massive, sliding door. Grasping the handle, he ushered the enormous panel from left to right until the entirety of it, except the metal ring he had hold of, disappeared inside the wall. Reaching inside, he flicked a switch. Instantly, the massive room was bathed in brilliant, white light. "Here is the first part of your new army," he remarked, sweeping out a beefy hand in dramatic fashion. "I still have minor modifications to make to them, though, but it shouldn't take long at all."

"What sort of modifications? And what do you mean by 'the first part' of my army? There's more?"

The girth of the gentleman's belly shook as he laughed. "I've been instructed by your master to alter their programming, so they will accept verbal commands from you. As for what I meant, the machines you see before you are the most substantial part of the army, but I've also been commanded to release your friends from service so that they may travel with you," the supervisor replied, nodding his head toward the impish creatures that Verin loathed.

Great! I've been saddled with a bunch of annoying cowards who will probably be more irritating than helpful! Shaking his head in disgust, Verin turned to regard the row upon row of machines that would soon be at his disposal. He was amazed by the multitude of dormant sentinels which covered every square inch of the floor before him; the mechanical minions ranging in size from the tiny, beetle-like creatures, to rats and bats, to large cats resembling mountain lions. Even larger still, were the giant, humanoid machines which resembled trolls. These later machines dwarfed anything Verin had encountered in the past, including the cyborgs in the abandoned city below the mountain and the mechanical horses that his adversaries rode. "How long do you expect the reprogramming to take?"

The supervisor scrunched his face in thought, looking

over the array of machines before him. "I should be able to finish altering their programming within an hour or two," he remarked after calculating the number of creatures in the room and guessing about how long it would take to make the necessary changes to each one. Removing an object from his pocket, the man held it out toward Verin. "One last thing. I need you to speak into this device in order to capture your voice so I can make the proper adjustments."

Nodding, Verin complied with the supervisor's request. "I'll be right outside, near the river. When you finish, come get me." Leaving the man to his work, he drifted through the exit and into the tunnel.

As Verin waited impatiently for the stocky human to complete the modifications to his new army, he paced back and forth down the corridor flanking the underground river. If the tiny, impish demons that comprised the Factory's workforce had been less annoying, he might have stayed inside and conversed with them to pass the time. Thankfully, the supervisor's estimate had been fairly accurate. The man was strolling through the doorway into the tunnel right now, hopefully to let him know the army was ready.

"Your legions await your commands," he announced with a smile.

Chapter 21

Exhausted from traveling for days on very little rest, Edward decided enough was enough. With the abandoned town a safe distance behind them, and the fact they had encountered nothing more dangerous than the woodland animals they hunted for food, he halted their progress in a small clearing. "I don't know about the rest of you, but I can barely keep my eyes open," he announced, hopping down from the steed he shared with Brian.

"I thought you would never say that." Katie smiled weakly, emitting a barely audible sigh. She could tell that most of Edward's wounds had healed from the intense battle a few days ago, mainly by the way he carried himself, but also because she had noticed the difference in his energy and enthusiasm. If she didn't know better, Katie would think he was almost as good as new. Even Julie was recovering from her captivity at an alarming rate. Other than her friend not being the chatterbox she once was, everything else about her seemed back to normal. Her pallor no longer appeared sickly, her voice wasn't scratchy anymore, and with all the nourishment she had been taking in that she'd previously been deprived of, her sagging skin had filled out and erased the emaciated look she had when they found her.

No further encouragement was needed. Before any of them could say another word, everyone had dismounted.

Brian had even gone so far as to wander off into the nearby forest to collect firewood. If it weren't for the fact that she was so weary she could barely stand, Katie would likely have followed the shaman and done a little hunting.

Within a matter of fifteen minutes, Brian returned to the clearing with an armload of wood. Placing the branches and twigs on the ground, he deftly arranged a good portion of his haul and Edward did the honors of igniting the fire. Tired beyond imagining, they quickly wrapped themselves in the blankets they had acquired from the abandoned town and encircled the campfire, lying down in the partially green grass as the sun hung low in the sky and cast a red-orange hue over everything. There were a few mumblings about setting a watch, but Edward seemed content to rely on Brian's heightened awareness of evil, figuring it would give them enough warning if danger should happen to stroll into their neck of the woods. Before drifting off to sleep, the last thing Katie heard was the soft, familiar sound of moving water.

Unsure of how long she had slept, Katie opened her eyes to almost total darkness. The campfire had almost completely gone out, leaving only traces of an orange glow emanating from its embers. Sitting up, she probed the immediate area with her fingers in search of the remaining pile of wood Brian had gathered. After a minute, she located the branches and grasped a few pieces to add to the fire before the chilly night air extinguished it completely. When the flames began to lick at the dried twigs and ignite, she stoked the fire, adding more and more wood until the spreading warmth caused her to back up a few feet.

The infusion of heat stirred the others to wakefulness. Rubbing his eyes, Edward sat up and glanced skyward. His brows crinkled into a frown when he didn't see either of the moons in the veil of darkness above him. *Did I sleep that long?* It was strange for him to sleep through an entire cycle of the brilliant, white orbs rising and setting, but it seemed like he had done just that. It left him feeling disoriented.

"What's wrong?" Katie asked, seeing the confused look on his face.

Shaking his head, he turned to meet her gaze. "Nothing, I guess," he shrugged. "It just felt weird for a second, not seeing one or both of the moons overhead."

"Maybe the first one hasn't come up yet," Katie surmised.

"Somehow, I doubt it. My body feels like I've slept far too long for that to be true."

"I don't know about the rest of you, but to me it almost seems like the sun should be out," Brian interjected with a half-hearted laugh.

One eyebrow crept up Katie's forehead as a barely audible sound distracted her from the conversation. "Shhh," she whispered, putting her index finger to her lips. Cocking her head to one side, she strained to decipher the noise. "Does anyone else hear that?" Her eyes flitted from one face to another, looking for any indication that any of them heard what she did.

"I don't hear anything," Edward remarked.

"Nor do I," Brian added. "But …"

"But, what?" Katie pried.

"I'm getting a faint sense of something," he answered. "It seems to be coming from above us."

"Well, I'll tell you what I hear. It sounds like flapping wings, and large ones at that." Katie looked up into the shroud of darkness that enveloped them. Worry lines creased her forehead and for a moment she almost expected something to swoop out of the night sky to attack them.

"I think I hear it, too," Julie whispered.

Suddenly, the veil of night was lifted for a few seconds. "Holy ... fucking ... shit!" Whipping her head up to gaze upon the anomaly, Katie saw an enormous streak of fire shooting northward through the sky. "What the hell was that?"

The sound of beating wings grew louder for a moment, but quickly receded. As did the conflagration above them. "Whatever it was, I think it may have been an ally," Brian stated softly. "The strange sense I was getting a short time ago is gone."

"Do you think it was one of the Gods, intervening on our behalf?" Katie asked, tapping Edward on the shoulder to get his attention.

"Divine intervention? I don't think so," he replied, shaking his head. "I can't be positive, though. All I can say is that I've never witnessed anything like that before."

For the next hour, the four of them sat around the campfire and swapped theories on the night's events. No further phenomenon occurred during their conversation, and Brian assured them that whatever had caused the sight they'd witnessed was long gone. Before any of them had realized just how much time they had spent discussing the possibilities, the first rays of morning light began to show on the horizon.

As the sky brightened, the topics of their conversations shifted toward the day ahead. "I've noticed that you've rebounded from your injuries quite well," Katie addressed Edward in a light-hearted tone. "I think Julie is in much better shape now as well."

"What are you getting at?" Curiously, Edward looked her way.

"While I know that you are likely feeling as if you could travel for another week on the amount of rest you got last night, I wanted to see if you would mind sticking around here for another day?"

"If you have a valid reason for staying here, I would certainly consider it before making the decision to leave."

"Well … um … for the past few days, I've been considering teaching Julie how to use my crossbow."

"Can't that wait? You know better than anyone how urgent our mission is," Edward retorted. "We have plenty of food at the moment, and someone can always help you load the bow if you need to hunt."

"True," Katie admitted, "but hunting isn't the only reason I'm asking." She paused for a second, allowing her words to sink in, and watched his eyebrow creep up into his hairline and disappear. "Until such time that my hand heals up enough to load the bow by myself, I think it would be beneficial to have another person in the group who can use it. Especially if the unexpected rears its ugly head out of nowhere. If I were forced to use the crossbow in battle, I would be as useless as a one-legged man in an ass kicking contest."

Although he was hesitant to concede that her observations were valid, he nodded his head in agreement. "Point taken. We will remain here for now, but only until sunrise tomorrow. It may not be enough time to show her every nuance, but it should be enough to make her competent with the weapon. I'm certainly not going to expect her to acquire your skill level in a day."

Wearing an ear to ear grin, Katie crawled across the ground to where Edward sat and planted a big, wet kiss on his cheek. "Thank you!"

Chapter 22

Once the initial surge of excitement passed—after acquiring his new toy he had flown recklessly through the sky as if he were joyriding down the streets back home in a beefed-up muscle car—George steered his mount in increasingly larger circles, hoping to catch a glimpse of the group he was sent to find. When the sun began to rise on that first day, and his efforts had produced nothing, he guided the beast to the ground to take cover during the daylight hours as he'd been instructed. Not that he cared about following the Black Knight's orders. It just made things easier for him, knowing he would have to catch the demon by surprise if he ever wanted to get his revenge.

Though the cooler air of the higher elevations had exhilarated and invigorated him, not to mention the frigid temperatures stopping the flow of blood from his leg wounds, he quickly became bored after hopping from his steed's back. With nothing better to do for the time being, he sat down at the base of a barren maple tree, tucked his fingers together behind his head, leaned back against the trunk, and drifted off to sleep.

When George awoke later that afternoon, he stretched and stood, gazing toward the bright yellow orb in the sky. If he was correct, he assumed there was only an hour or two of daylight left. For the first time since his departure from the mountain, he felt and heard his stomach rumble. Shuffling through the dead leaves, he approached his metallic steed. Pushing the button behind the foreleg that the Black Knight had shown him, he ascended the steps and removed the pack of supplies from the lever. Hopping to the ground again, he opened the sack to see what sort of goodies the demon had seen fit to give him.

Digging through the bag, he pulled out a handful of what looked to be dried meat of some sort, though it was shriveled and white so he couldn't be absolutely certain. Knotting the sack shut, he draped the drawstring over the control lever of his mount and sat down next to the tree he had been napping under.

Placing his stash in his lap, George picked up a strip of the strange looking meat and held it under his nose. Taking a tentative sniff, he noticed nothing unusual about the smell. In fact, it didn't appear to have a scent at all! Cautiously, he ripped a small portion from the strip with his teeth, rolled the meat around in his mouth for a few seconds, then began chewing. As was the case when he had sniffed it moments ago, the flavor was nondescript. The first thing which came to mind was that it tasted like chicken, but wasn't it usually what people thought when they tasted something so bland?

Even though the meat was nothing to write home about, he continued eating until his stomach ceased its rumblings. George let his thoughts wander as he ate, thinking about the coming night's patrol and hoping for success. Closing his eyes, he daydreamed about what he would do if he actually found the small group tonight. A distant commotion, sounding as if it were getting steadily closer to his position, roused him from his thoughts. Tilting his head, he listened, carefully attempting to discern which direction the noise was coming from.

It was difficult to be absolutely sure, but the cacophony seemed to be approaching from the north. Which, if memory served was the direction of the abandoned town he'd seen at the base of the mountain; the same enormous hill where he had stood sentry outside of the blood red lighted cavern in which the Black Knight held his captives in blasphemous crucifixion.

As the sun began to duck under the horizon, leaving him less light to view the possible threat inching ever closer to him, he narrowed his eyes and squinted toward the sound. It was definitely drawing nearer, and he had increasingly more trouble deciphering what was approaching. The mixture of noises began to hurt his ears. There seemed to be an underlying clicking, the din of which was almost like listening to the clatter of silverware. Above that, a steadier, whirring fracas, much like a propeller of some sort, the resonance bearing a similarity to a small airplane preparing to take flight.

The bedlam drew closer still, and George began to see movement, barely perceptible, but unmistakably moving toward him. Through the haze of dust, which almost appeared like a giant cloud of fog, he could see enormous trees, tilting crazily and toppling to the earth. He started to notice the slight trembling of the ground beneath him, and he knew the steadily marching giants, with glints of the fading sunlight reflecting off them, were the cause of it. From this distance, he couldn't tell just how big these creatures were, but if his eyes weren't deceiving him, he thought they may be as large as twelve feet tall! Maybe it was a trick of the lighting, but it appeared that these huge beings were swatting trees out of their way as if they were a child's set of Tinkertoys.

Panic began to set in to his mind. *Did the Black Knight sense my deception outside of Cemetery Hill? Did he trick me into believing I had his trust, knowing full well that he intended to send his armies to destroy me?* Casting a nervous glance toward his steed, he couldn't help but wonder if he should flee before the encroaching army reached his position. *Do I dare to stick around and find out?* A resounding, *No!* echoed through his head.

Forgetting about the remnants of meat still sitting in his lap, George stood, the coarse white strips of jerky falling to the ground at his feet. He didn't relish the idea of running away like a coward, but he knew the odds were heavily against him if he stood his ground. Quickly, he ascended to the back of his steed, remembering to move his legs before he depressed the black button to extend the creature's wings. Within seconds, he was airborne.

As the three-headed, winged, demonic monstrosity rose above the treetops, George steered it in a slow circle to get a better look at the forces arrayed against him. When he saw just how massive the army truly was, he thanked his common sense for telling him to flee. He couldn't tell for sure how big the assemblage was because the sun had dipped below the horizon, its light no longer reflecting from the metallic shells of the creatures below, but he was certain the force was enormous. Where the army was positioned there were no trees to obstruct his view, almost as if the machines were obliterating everything in their path.

Determined to get as far from the army below as he could, George turned his steed to the south. Fifteen minutes later, he swiveled his head and glanced behind him. When he noticed he could no longer see the army, or the trail of death they blazed as they marched forward, George sighed and started to relax. Spinning his face into the wind, he took several calming breaths as the cool air caressed his skin and blew his long, brown hair out straight behind him as if he had suddenly grown a tail on the back of his skull. At the moment, nothing mattered to him except putting as much distance between himself and the Black Knight's army as he could. Finding the small group of people seemed irrelevant. The only thing George cared about right now was living to see another day.

Feeling the wind rush through his ears like a howling demon, George sped through the night sky without a care in the world. He didn't concern himself with the Black Knight's mission, not even bothering to look below him. If he had, George might have seen the flickering of a campfire. Instead, he allowed his head to tilt back so he could gaze upon the unfamiliar stars overhead, to take in the beauty of his freedom.

It was during this short span of time, while he felt the cool, night air melting his worries away, that he first heard the sound. Initially, he had scanned the area in front of him, thinking the noise may have been the rumblings of a thunder cloud, but as he peered into the darkness he doubted it was what he had heard. Only a multitude of twinkling stars dotted his vision. There wasn't a single cloud in sight, let alone a thunderhead.

When he heard the noise again, a few seconds later, he realized that it wasn't a storm approaching, but something else. If he wasn't mistaken, the steady thrum of turbulence in the air reminded him of a bird flapping its wings. He scoffed at the notion. *There is no way a bird could create a noise of that depth. It would have to be as big as a house.* Before he could entirely dismiss the idea, George noticed a large section of the stars he'd been admiring a moment ago disappear before his eyes.

Keeping his focus on the darkened section of sky, he turned his steed to the left in a slow arc. Before he had time to think, the veil of night was broken by what appeared to be a giant fireball. It streaked through the darkness toward him, giving George only a second or two to react. Slapping the control lever hard to the left, his steed veered sharply in that direction. He felt his body slide, threatening to eject him from the creature's back. Clamping his thighs together as tight as he could, George grasped at anything he could get his hands on to keep from falling to his death. His fingertips found purchase in a crease of metal in the beast's shiny hide, allowing him a brief moment to steady his mount.

He could still hear his adversary's enormous wings beating the air into submission behind him and to his right. Slowly, George moved the control lever of his steed until it was upright again. The normally cold, night air around him was anything but normal. Though the wind rushing into his face was cool, he could feel a hot breeze against his back. Knowing the flying giant was likely right behind him, he pushed his mount's control lever forward. Gradually adding more pressure to the stick, the beast descended toward the ground. It was the only option George could think of right now. He only hoped that whatever was chasing him through the sky wouldn't follow him to the ground.

The journey through the tunnels from the Factory, into Cemetery Hill, and finally to the outside world had been tedious at best, but after several trips upon the railcar to the base of the mountain, Verin was at last able to assemble his new army into one, giant column for the march south. It had been early morning by the time the large formation was ready to get underway, but once they began moving, Verin was more than pleased with the rapidity of their progress. The machines devoured everything in their path. Buildings were reduced to rubble. The dying grasses were trampled to dust. Trees were toppled and pulverized, blazing a path of destruction as they steadily marched toward their objective.

One thing Verin had discovered in his short command over his mechanical counterparts was that communication with his troops was a two way street. He had only expected his new minions to obey his instructions. Little had he known that he would be able to decipher the clicks and clacks of their mechanized speech. It certainly aided his ability to guide them. It was an added bonus when he discovered that he could hold simple conversations with the machines, almost as if they were intelligent enough to think for themselves.

As the day wore on, he was increasingly thankful of his subordinates. One of the giant, troll-like sentinels had relayed information to him which apprised him of a potential threat ahead. If Verin understood the machine correctly, it was entirely possible that his army had discovered the group of mortals the Black Knight had sent them to destroy. It didn't appear likely to him, though. The humans had a few days head start on them, and it didn't seem probable that they would dally so close to the mountain.

Nonetheless, the giant machine had told him of a nearby mechanical signature. Possibly one of the two-headed, horse-like creatures that Verin knew was their only method of expedient travel. As the column marched inexorably forward, he thought he saw a glint of light reflecting from something ahead. Before they were able to get close enough to investigate the source, an interesting thing happened.

The shiny object rapidly rose into the sky, gleaming with the last, dying light of the sun's rays and streaking away from the column of machines. Verin knew when he saw it that the creature he'd seen was not one of the horse-like beasts, but before he could consider its true identity and purpose, one of the giant trolls told him the mechanical signature had disappeared.

Letting out a harsh sigh of frustration because his prey had managed to elude him, Verin started the army forward once again. *You can run, but you can't hide. I will find you again if I have to travel to the edge of this forsaken world.*

Chapter 23

Katie was excited. After Edward had agreed to give her the day to instruct Julie on how to use her crossbow, she had found her once dainty friend more than capable of wielding the weapon. Perhaps the most difficult task associated with the usage of the bow was getting the drawstring pulled back so it could be loaded. At first, Katie was unsure if Julie had the upper body strength, but was pleasantly surprised that she was able to accomplish it with fluid ease after the first couple of attempts.

Once Katie was certain her friend could load the crossbow with near combat quickness, she moved on to teaching her how to aim and fire the weapon. For the first couple of hours, Katie gave tips and pointers on how to improve her accuracy, picking out a stationary object for a target and having Julie take shots at it. When she was satisfied with Julie's progress, she took her lessons one step further. Despite her friend's protestations about shooting at living beings, Katie took her into the surrounding forest to hunt, hoping Julie would adapt to targeting an unpredictable, moving target as well as she had the stationary ones during practice. This was the closest thing she could offer her friend to simulate combat. It was just an added bonus if her lessons were successful and they returned to camp with an abundance of fresh meat. If nothing else, it would mean they could skip hunting for a while.

The two women returned to camp later that afternoon, laughing and carrying on as if they had never been apart. As they walked toward the fire, Katie lifted Julie's arm high in the air, a string of trophy rabbits spinning in crazy circles from the twine wrapped around her fist.

"I think she's got the hang of it," Katie announced, a smile so wide crossing her features that her lips looked like they were trying to nibble on her ears.

"Holy cow!" Brian remarked in awe as he glanced toward them.

"Holy cow is right," Edward agreed. "It's going to take us all night to cook them."

"Well, hop to it. Get it? Hop? Rabbit?" Katie laughed hysterically at the wry smile on Edward's face as he shook his head.

"I thought you said he had a sense of humor?" Julie whispered, cupping her hand over Katie's ear.

Never taking her eyes off Edward, she responded to her friend's query. "Oh, he does. He just doesn't like to show it all the time. He thinks that nobody will take him seriously if he's always joking around. At least, that's my opinion."

As they sat around the evening fire, the last rabbit cooking over the flames and their bellies almost uncomfortably full, the pervading mood of the group was more jovial than Katie had seen in her entire time on Desolace. In the past hour she had heard more laughter and jokes than any time in recent memory, and it warmed her heart. Maybe, just maybe, things would turn out all right. Though thoughts of their journey ahead weren't far from their minds, for the time being at least, they had been able to focus on more mundane things and develop even stronger bonds with one another than any of them had considered possible.

When all the meat was cooked, and stored safely inside the hollowed chest of Brian's steed to keep the enticing aroma from attracting predators from the forest, their conversations began to wane. From where Katie sat, it looked to her as if the telltale signs of *fat puppy syndrome* were putting a stranglehold on everyone. As she glanced from face to face in the diminishing firelight, she saw the heavy, drooping eyelids, and the seemingly vacant look in the eyes of each of her companions.

Absently, Edward grabbed a few larger branches and gently placed them in the fire. A brief shower of sparks fluttered toward the night sky as his mouth stretched open in a cavernous yawn. "I don't know about all of you, but I can't keep my eyes open."

With the night winding down, Katie sighed and leaned back, spreading her blanket out and preparing to lay down. "Ditto."

"No watch tonight?" Brian rubbed his eyelids and gazed toward Edward.

"No. I think we can rely on your senses. There hasn't been anything since the fireball in the sky last night to indicate we could be in any danger. Besides, everyone needs to get as much rest as possible. We get back underway tomorrow."

"You don't need to tell us twice." Katie grinned sleepily, tucking an arm under her head and closing her eyes. Feeling Julie's arm drape over her midsection, she scooted backward a few inches, until she felt the warmth of her friend's body pressing against her back, then let out a contented sigh.

When the women awoke the next morning to the sound of stomping feet, they sat up quickly, startled. They relaxed when they saw the source of the noise, Edward, tapping his boots on the dying embers of their campfire to make sure it was fully extinguished before they left. Brian was standing near the mechanical horses, apparently making sure that all of their supplies were loaded properly and secure.

"Well, well, well. Our resident sleepyheads are finally awake," Brian joked when he saw Katie and Julie sitting up, still encased in their blankets as if they were butterflies preparing to emerge from their cocoons.

"Very funny, Carrot Top," Katie remarked, waving a dismissive hand at the shaman as she stood.

"Who?" Edward frowned in confusion.

"Never mind, Edward. You wouldn't understand. Carrot Top was a comedian where Julie and I are from."

Shaking his head, he turned his attention back to his task. *One of these days I may actually understand more of her offhand references, but I doubt it will be any time soon. Hopefully, we live long enough for that day to come.*

Katie escorted Julie to their steed and opened its chest to stash their blankets. Thankfully, she had grown more accustomed to the strange creatures, and although she still seemed hesitant around them, she no longer appeared to be fearful of them.

Once their bedding was stowed, Katie returned to where she'd slept last night and looked at the ground in confusion. "Has anyone seen the crossbow?"

"It's behind the saddle of your mount," Brian replied. "Sorry, I was just trying to make sure we didn't forget anything."

"Thanks! I was freaking out for a second there. Thought something had snuck up on us last night and dragged it off into the woods."

Over the course of the next several hours, Brian maneuvered his metallic steed through the steadily thickening, leafless trees. Whether it was by fate or accident, they had, once again, found the river which ran north to south across the northernmost regions of Desolace. As they rode beside the gently moving waters, Edward informed them that the tributary followed the range of mountains to their east and would eventually dump into the ocean at the edge of the known world. He told the others that there were rumors of land masses beyond the sea, and if the legends he'd heard as a child were true, there was a ghostly ship which patrolled the waters. Whether the boat cruised the ocean in search of passengers to escort to the rumored southern lands, or if it were a sentinel positioned to keep men in the northern regions, he couldn't say for certain. The only thing he *could* tell them was that they would find out for sure if they ever reached the shores of the ocean.

Glancing skyward, Edward was thankful that they had found the river again. Dark clouds scuttled across the heavens, obscuring the sun. He couldn't help but wonder if the foreboding murk above them was an attempt, by the dark forces they fought against, to confuse their sense of direction and cause them to travel in impotent circles. If it was the case, it no longer mattered. The gentle current to their left would be their guide.

As the afternoon wore on, the gloom sank ever closer. The billowing bellies of the darkened clouds looking fatter by the minute, as if the threat of a torrential downpour was in the immediate future. Keeping a close eye on the weather, they picked their way through the tangles of underbrush that dotted the western bank of the river. After another hour of riding, it was getting obvious that they should consider stopping. Even though they couldn't see the sun's position, the growing darkness was indicating the fact that night time would soon swallow them up.

Finding a decent spot to set up camp, they dismounted and went about their preparations. There was an abundance of meat still stored in the cavernous chest of Brian's steed, so Katie and Julie helped with the gathering of firewood. Edward cleared a place for their campfire while the others wandered into the nearby tree line, though they never left his sight. Apparently, fallen limbs were in abundant supply. In a matter of minutes, the three gatherers returned, each of them bearing a huge armload of timber. So much, in fact, that Edward surmised they could build a beacon of fire the Gods would notice.

Once the fire was started, Katie and Julie retrieved the blankets from their steed, and Brian rummaged through their food supplies. After the bedding and their evening meal was distributed, the four weary travelers made idle conversation as they ate.

Chewing the last morsel of cold, rabbit meat, Edward whipped his head around when he heard a disturbance behind him. Barely visible, the firelight reflected off several droplets of water, which rose from the river like rain trying to return home to the clouds overhead. At first he was unable to comprehend the phenomenon, but the cause soon revealed itself to him.

"Long time, no see," a watery voice floated up from the river.

"Indeed, it is good to see that you still live," another garbled voice commented.

"Is that who I think it is?" Katie tapped Edward on the shoulder to get his attention.

"It certainly sounds like it," he replied without turning. "Kronos? Kieron? Is that you?" Rising to his feet, Edward strolled casually to the edge of the river with Katie on his heels. Julie glanced toward Brian with a confused look. In return, the shaman merely shrugged his shoulders and twirled his index finger around in circles beside his head.

Clapping a hand over her mouth, Julie snickered.

Scanning the river's surface, Edward located his two-headed friend bobbing in the current a few feet from shore. "How are you, friend? What brings you to these parts? Still searching for warmer waters perhaps?"

"I am fine. Although less frigid temperatures would be nice, it is not my main concern right now," Kronos replied.

"I've been searching for you. I have urgent news," Kieron added.

Katie stifled a giggle as the thought of a fish-o-gram floated through her mind.

After throwing a quick frown in her direction, Edward returned his focus to the river. "What news do you bring? And, please don't tell me that there's an evil man riding a mechanical beast heading in our direction."

"That would be a blessing, I'm afraid," Kronos admitted, his head dipping toward the water.

"Indeed," Kieron agreed. "My news is much worse than that."

"Worse?" Worry lines creased Edward's forehead and his eyebrows rose dramatically.

"Much worse," Kieron sighed. "One man riding a machine is bad, but what comes for you now is far more lethal. There is an enormous army of metal creatures heading this way. They are scouring the area to find you, and with a force that large it can only spell one thing. Death."

Chapter 24

Thankfully, whatever had tried to kill him a short time ago had not followed him to the ground, though, George could still hear the steady whoosh of the creature's wings beating the air above him. Despite the fact that he felt like a coward for running away, he surmised it to be better to wait until daylight so he could see what he was up against. Attempting another confrontation in the dark would be suicide, although, once he discovered what sort of beast was after him, he may come to the same conclusion. The only thing he could do now was wait. Moving his steed toward a giant pine, he dismounted once he was certain the creature was sufficiently camouflaged.

Lying down on a bed of pine needles beneath the tree, he laced his fingers together behind his head. Though he thought sleep would elude him tonight, he let out a long breath, closed his eyes, and listened to the rhythmic beat of the monstrous wings. Within fifteen minutes, his heartbeat slowed and he was embraced by the bliss of slumber.

Initially, George had thought he was dreaming, but when the Black Knight's seething voice broke the silence for a second time, he sat up quickly, as if someone had jolted him with an electric shock. Disoriented, he rubbed and blinked his eyes.

For the third time, the demon's voice erupted from somewhere nearby, sounding even more agitated than his last inquiry. "Have you found them yet?"

"Not yet," George responded, glancing nervously in every direction and expecting to see the cloaked figure burning a hole through him with its fierce, yellow eyes. When he couldn't locate the demon, he stood and brushed the pine needles from his clothes. Walking across the uneven ground, George approached his mount to get something to eat.

"Well, get busy! If you don't find them soon, there is a chance they could escape."

The Black Knight's voice was so loud it felt as if he were standing right next to him, shouting in George's ear. For a moment, George thought that somehow the demon was inside his head, but he dismissed the idea when he considered the possibility of more than one spiritual force being inside the same fleshy cover. Then, where did the voice come from? Patiently, he considered his next words, hoping to keep up the illusion of being the younger version of himself. "How can they escape? Is there one of those portal thingies around, like the one you brought me through?"

"I don't know how," the Black Knight growled, drawing George's attention to one of the three massive heads of his steed.

Is he speaking through the machine?

"And you need not concern yourself with those details. Find them! When you do, let me know so I can inform my army of their whereabouts."

Hearing the Black Knight's final instructions brought about a sudden shift in George's demeanor, relaxing as he realized that what he had seen yesterday was not an ill-conceived attempt at deception, but rather the muscle to ensure the destruction of the humans he was looking for.

With his mind at ease about yesterday's events, George questioned the demon about the nearly fatal incident of the previous evening. "Do you have any idea what was chasing me through the sky last night?"

"Probably an illusion cast by the wizard. You must have been close to discovering their position."

"Excuse me? I hardly believe it was a spell. I felt like I was being chased by a flamethrower with wings. It maintained pursuit far beyond my initial contact with it. If it were an illusion, as you suggest, it would have vanished into thin air when it reached a certain distance from the spell caster." He hoped he was right. The only thing he based his comment on was the years he had spent playing *Dungeons & Dragons* as a kid.

The ensuing growl that emanated from one of the three heads of his steed warned George of the demon's growing impatience. "Is this mythical beast still visible?"

"It was still circling overhead when I fell asleep last night, but it appears to be gone now."

"Then, quit worrying about something that isn't there! Grow some balls and do your damn job!"

"Fine," George spat, suddenly wishing he could sever the mechanical head the demon was speaking through.

"Don't get testy with me, boy! Remember your place! You are a fly upon this insignificant shit pile you call life, and I'm the flyswatter! Cross me and you will regret it for the rest of your miserable life!"

After refusing to dignify the Black Knight's threats with a response, George had paced back and forth for the last two hours, wearing a trenched groove in the earth beneath the pine needles he had slept upon. Muttering to himself, his eyebrows furrowed so deeply they became one with each other, making him look like a Neanderthal. His eyes narrowed to slits, as he began plotting his vengeance against the demon who sought to control him. His thoughts were muddled at first, but as he stalked the area around his mount like a crazed bird on the track of a cuckoo clock, an idea began to form.

The Black Knight had mentioned an army sent to destroy the humans George was looking for. *What if, after I find the group and relay the information back to him so he can notify his forces on where to concentrate their attack, he decides to turn his legions on me? And, what if I were to convince his own minions to retaliate against their master after dispatching the humans? Is it even possible to persuade them with their own freedom? To no longer have a master other than themselves?*

Stopping beside his three headed mount, George patted the nearest neck with a wicked grin. There was only one way to find out. Since the Black Knight had not seen the thing which chased him through the sky last night, he was relatively sure there was no way he could see what he was about to do. Even though there still appeared to be a few hours of daylight left, George mounted his metallic steed and took to the air.

An hour later, his search yielded results. Far below him was the obvious swath of destruction caused by the Black Knight's enormous army, looking like an elongated, filthy penis wearing a shiny, metal condom. Even from this height, George could tell the legion of machines likely numbered in the thousands. For that matter, there could be hundreds of thousands. The cloud of dust and debris rising from the marching column acted like a shroud of fog. George was fairly certain the haze below was no accident, but rather a means to mask the true size of the regiment.

Deciding to move in for a closer inspection before making actual contact, George pushed the control lever forward about halfway, sending his mount into a swooping dive. Once he was near enough to make out finer details on the large, troll-like machines bringing up the rear of the column, he allowed the lever to snap back into its original, upright position. Circling the large assemblage of machines like a hawk scouting its prey, he scanned the masses in search of a leader.

Having suspected for a short time that the Black Knight himself might be leading the army, George was pleasantly surprised to find his initial suspicions had been wrong. Instead of the cloaked demon at the head of the column, there was a wispy, nearly insubstantial, ghost-like form. When he'd lain eyes on it the first time, he had thought it to be a dusty mirage. Now that he was closer, he knew that it wasn't the case. *There's something different about this ghost, though. When I'm outside of the confines of a body during the daylight hours, I'm invisible to the naked eye. This one is not. It almost looks like a human, shaped from the vapors of fog. Substantial enough that I can't see through it, but constantly shifting its appearance as if it were no more real than a puff of smoke.*

George continued to circle the massive force, careening through the air like a fighter pilot, skimming just above the treetops. After a few minutes, he realized the haze surrounding the machines was thinning. *They stopped!* If his eyes weren't playing tricks on him, the entire metallic army had raised their heads to the sky, looking at him. For a brief moment, he was worried. Thoughts of laser beams, bursting from their eye sockets and blasting toward him, weighed heavily on his mind. After a few tense seconds, nothing happened, and he scoffed at himself for being foolish. *This ain't a fucking Star Trek movie, dumb ass!*

Testing a theory, he dipped his steed lower still, zipping over their heads at a height he assumed would be out of reach of the giant machines at the rear of the column. The massive creatures made no move to attack him, and none of the smaller mechanisms seemed to stir either. It was almost as if someone had flicked a switch and turned the entire field of metallic sentinels off. As George flew closer, tempting fate should he be wrong about the intentions of the machines or their leader, he was amazed by the overwhelming variety of creatures represented in the army. It was like getting a sneak peek into a futuristic zoo. As amusing as that might sound, though, he had no desire to attempt petting any of the formidable beasts. For that matter, even though the mass of metal below him looked docile right now, he wasn't even entertaining thoughts of landing his steed. After all, it could be a trick; a way to lull him into their web of deceit. *No, thank you. I'll keep my happy ass up here in relative safety.*

Spotting the hazy form of the apparent leader again, which was easier now that the dust cloud had settled, George maneuvered his three headed mount toward the head of the column. Hovering in the air a few feet above Verin, an echoing, hollow voice greeted him.

"You seem familiar," the formless one intoned with a curious cock of his head. "Do I know you?"

"I've never met you before. My name is George." At the mention of his name, the ghostly form below him seemed to shift its stance. If he wasn't mistaken, the creature appeared agitated by his revelation. "And, who might you be?"

"I am Verin," he spat in disgust. *Isn't this the same asshole that the Black Knight sent me to destroy? He's supposed to be dead!* "I am the Black Knight's second in command, and the leader of his armies." He studied George's reaction to his announcement, wondering how the man's corpse could be so lively.

Appearing to reflect on Verin's words, George frowned and rubbed his chin. "I, too, am working for the same entity," he admitted. "Perhaps we have the same goals and can help each other."

"Me ... help you?" Verin scoffed at the notion. "If you are truly one of my master's disciples you can aid me, but I will *not* return the favor. Too many of the Black Knight's supposed followers have their own hidden agendas and I will not tolerate being deceived."

"Let me assure you, I have no such intentions," George lied. "I believe we have been tasked with similar missions. Perhaps, if I can help you accomplish your goals, you can put a good word in for me with the Black Knight."

Though he tried his best, Verin could not hide his amusement. "How do you propose to do that?" The formless demon laughed at the audacity of the mortal.

"Well, it seems to me that your army is restricted to the ground. I, however, am not." He gestured to his mount. "I can serve as a scout and help you locate your objective."

"What makes you think that we need your so-called help?"

"I'm not implying that you do, but I know it would speed up your search. If nothing else, my services would help keep you on track to your target instead of blindly blundering through the forest and hoping you find the nuisance you were tasked to destroy." When the ghost-like form below him did not immediately reply, George knew he had finally struck a cord and shown his potential value to the army.

"Fine," Verin sighed after a minute's hesitation. "Don't you dare cross me, though. I will turn this army on you in the blink of an eye if you give me a single reason to doubt your sincerity."

Chapter 25

After receiving the disturbing news from Kronos and Kieron, Edward and Katie returned to the campfire to relay the information to their friends. At first, Brian and Julie had trouble digesting the disclosure. Especially when they considered the source the report had come from. A talking, two-headed fish? Julie remembered the fish stories her father used to tell her when she was young, but this seemed completely outrageous. Once the idea of a creature like that being real began to set in, her initial disbelief wavered. *This isn't Earth. I've seen some pretty strange things on this world, so who's to say what is and is not possible here?*

Nervously, the four of them discussed their options. Though the flames of the fire between them warmed their skin, none of them were immune to the shivers and goosebumps that erupted across their flesh. If what Edward told them was true, they had to do something to throw their enemies off their trail for a while. At the very least to buy time for an escape. *Preferably someplace not on this crazy world,* Julie thought.

Once the awful reality of what lay ahead of them began to sink in fully, grim expressions adorned their faces as the shadows created by the firelight danced over their features. Not one of them dared to speak their mind, fearing that if they voiced their thoughts it would be like setting out the welcome mat for their own demise. The silence of the night air around them grew, thickening like a suffocating blanket of dense fog.

Their thoughts were heavy with the sense of impending doom, and sleep did not come easily for any of them. Even so, they eventually succumbed to slumber's embrace one by one because of their weariness, though it was far from restful. Nightmarish visions of being tortured and ripped apart by unseen tormentors plagued them, the disturbing images flickering across the insides of their eyelids like the previews of horror movies.

About an hour after drifting off, the resonance of a distant crash in the forest startled Katie awake. Disoriented, she sat up and rubbed her eyes with the back of a hand, wincing when she realized she was doing so with her broken extremity. *I really wish this damn thing would hurry up and heal.* When the sound did not immediately repeat, she began to wonder if it had been part of her dream. A minute went by, then two. Just as she was about to dismiss the noise as part of a nightmare and lay down again, another thud erupted in the distance.

Panic surfaced in her mind as Kronos' warning blotted out all other thoughts. Glancing nervously around the dying embers of the campfire, Katie looked to see if any of the others had heard what she had. Though their features were contorted by the nearly non-existent light, making it impossible to tell for certain if any of their eyes were open, she surmised that she was the only one awake. None of her companions so much as twitched.

As she was about to reach out and shake Edward's blanket, she caught movement from the corner of her eye.

Turning toward it, Katie almost cried out in relief. A ghostly form was rapidly approaching through the barren wasteland of hibernating trees, and somehow she knew it was Amber. It had been what seemed like forever since the last time Katie had seen her, and suddenly she felt like she'd never been happier to see someone in her life. Well, other than when she had found Julie, that is.

When the specter stopped before her, the ghostly form pulsated as Katie had witnessed many times in the past. Normally, Amber's strobing effect was caused by fear. "You have to get out of here," she warned. "There is a massive army of machines heading this way, and unbelievably enough … the bastard who killed me is leading the charge."

Katie's mouth dropped open in disbelief. "I—I thought he was dead," she stammered, the sound of alarm in her voice waking her sleeping friends.

"I thought so, too, but I know what I saw. I can't explain it. I've seen his essence roaming around, as if he were in the same predicament I'm in, but …"

"But, what?" Katie inquired, more confused than ever.

"If he really is a spirit, he has learned how to possess the living. The thing that makes it even creepier is the body he now resides in. It looks just like his old body, but somehow it's younger in appearance."

"What is all the commotion about?" Edward sat up groggily, still swaddled in his blanket. When his eyes focused on Amber's glowing form, he wasn't sure whether to be happy or frightened. It seemed like every time he saw the ghostly woman that something really bad was looming on the horizon, usually involving a grievous injury or death.

"Amber came to warn us. She confirmed what Kronos and Kieron told us earlier, and after what I heard a few minutes ago I think we need to get the hell out of here as soon as possible," Katie remarked, turning to face the sorcerer.

As quickly as Amber had shown up in their camp, it had taken Brian a few moments for his senses to alert him to her presence. When the sensation finally registered in his brain, he sat straight up as if he had been poked with a cattle prod. Though his shamanic ability was telling him there was no immediate threat to his wellbeing, or to his friends, he spun his head around toward the intruder. He relaxed slightly when he saw Amber's familiar face. The same couldn't be said for Julie, who fainted at the sight of their ghostly visitor, remembering all too well the trouble she had gotten herself into when she was back on Earth after being visited by the ghost.

The intense look upon Katie's face quickly evaporated the haze of sleep from Edward's brain. "So, if Kronos, Kieron, and Amber are correct about the danger we are in, we need to figure out a course of action. Something that will keep us safe, but at the same time give us a chance to rid the world of the pestilence that these machines carry with them," he stated thoughtfully, glancing from face to face and hoping for someone to have an idea of some sort. "I'm open to suggestions," he added when his comments were greeted with silence.

"I've got nothing," admitted Brian. "I may be great at detecting the presence of evil, but the best I could do is advise you that going in a certain direction would be a bad idea." He offered a tight-lipped smile to them that looked more like a grimace of pain.

"I wouldn't call that nothing. Your counsel is always welcome and appreciated," Edward remarked.

"I'm not sure why, but I've been feeling a pull of sorts since encountering the younger version of my tormentor," Amber confided.

"Where is this pull telling you that you should go?" Katie questioned, her eyes returning to the ghost's pulsating glow.

Hesitantly, Amber lifted a nearly transparent finger and pointed toward the southwest.

"Well, I can't speak for everyone else, but if you're leading us away from the army of machines heading this way, I say it's as good a plan as any." Katie smiled weakly. "So, when do we leave? First thing in the morning, or would we be putting ourselves in danger by waiting that long?"

"In my opinion, we should leave as soon as possible. Preferably, now," Amber replied in a grave tone that said she would like nothing more than to distance herself from the menace with the haste of a fleeing rabbit.

Edward seemed lost in thought for a moment. *As much as I despise rushing off into the darkness, especially toward places I've never been before, I doubt Amber would lead us astray. She never has in the past, and she's given us no indication that she has been influenced by other forces.* "Let's gather our things and get moving, then." Edward sighed, suppressing a yawn.

The first light of Dawn was creeping onto the horizon. Their progress over the last few hours had seemed slow, all things considered. Normally, when Amber led the way, they covered a lot of ground, but the thick foliage hampered their traveling speed to what almost felt like a crawl. Even so, they had put a comfortable amount of distance between themselves and the approaching army. The distant crashing noises were far less menacing now, the sounds carrying to their ears like a gentle rustling of leaves.

With a sigh of despair, Katie realized they wouldn't have Amber's guidance for much longer. When the sun rose a little higher she would vanish from sight.

"What's wrong?" Edward halted the mount he and Brian shared and turned to regard Katie.

Instead of responding verbally, she pointed toward the rising sun and nodded her head toward Amber. It seemed to take a few seconds for her implication to register in the wizard's weary mind, but she soon saw in his eyes that he understood. "What do you want to do after sunrise? The last thing I want to do is hang out here all day, waiting for Amber to reappear, and give those machines a chance to catch up to us," Katie remarked.

While she was still visible, Amber lifted her arm and pointed. "Keep heading in that direction," she told them. "Even though you won't be able to see me, I promise to stay by your side until nightfall."

Thankfully, Amber had spoken up when she did, because the rapidly approaching sunrise had reduced her glowing form to the point where she looked like a mirage.

A minute later, she was gone entirely. Not even a shimmering trace of her remained visible.

"Well, I don't think you will like my opinion very much," Edward stated bluntly. "In my eyes, we should keep going until—"

"While I understand your reasoning for pushing everyone to their physical limits, I think it would be wise to at least stop from time to time," Katie interrupted. "Even if it is only for a quick meal and a short nap."

"She has a point, Edward. If we are tired and hungry we will be more likely to travel slower, not to mention the hallucinations that sleep deprivation would cause. It would be foolish to allow ourselves to get to that point, especially if the machines catch up to us and we are forced to engage them in battle," Brian added.

"Okay, okay. No need to get all uptight." Edward raised his hands in surrender. "I was merely sharing my thoughts on the matter. This isn't an autocracy, and I am not so bullheaded that I won't consider what everyone else thinks. Although most of you consider me to be your leader, I will not do so with an iron fist."

Despite her weariness, Katie couldn't help but laugh. "Since you put it *that* way, I vote to take our first break now." She grinned.

By the time the sun began to hang low in the cloudy sky, Katie was thankful for the cat naps she had managed to take throughout the day. If Edward hadn't agreed with her and forced them to soldier on, she would likely be an overly tired, mega-bitch right now. That was the last thing any of them wanted.

A fluffy, dark cloud scuttled across the deepening blue above them as evening rapidly approached, blotting out the fiery orb of the sun and allowing the hazy form of their ghostly friend to become slightly visible. Even though they could see Amber, she wasn't completely substantial. The biggest drawback of this state of being was that they couldn't hear her voice. She had to be fully transformed for her words to be audible. In this mirage-like form she could only communicate with gestures, making it similar to talking to a deaf person. Even so, Katie could tell that Amber was excited, or perhaps nervous, about something.

As she glanced around, trying to figure out what Amber was attempting to tell them, Katie realized for the first time just how creepy her surroundings looked. Though the forest around them was still dense with foliage, the wooden sentinels in the immediate area appeared different, somehow less lively. It made her think of a blighted graveyard, the landscape filled with things that were withered and dead. Her arms broke out in gooseflesh and a shiver crept up her spine, feeling like an icy finger was running along her backbone. Despite how much this section of forest was giving her the heebie-jeebies, her stomach rumbled loudly. "I don't relish the thought of hanging out here for long, but can we stop for a little bit and get something to eat?"

Tapping Brian on the shoulder, Edward spun his head around to face her as the shaman brought their mount to a stop. "Certainly," he smiled, "I'm feeling a bit famished myself."

Needing no further invitation, the four of them quickly dismounted. Opening up the panel on the chest of Brian's steed, Katie rummaged through their dwindling food supply. Julie and the two men huddled around her, holding out their hands like starving inmates who were standing in line at the prison kitchen. The metallic bands encircling Julie's wrists only added to this illusion. They accepted the food Katie passed to them and wolfed it down greedily, not bothering with idle chit chat or sitting down.

By the time the impromptu meal was finished, the sun was sinking below the horizon. With their bellies satisfied for the moment, the group mounted their metallic transportation and turned their eyes toward their ghostly friend. Amber was swiftly becoming more substantial. Once the sun had set, she almost appeared solid. Her glowing form was the only real indication that she wasn't.

"There is something nearby. I think it's the source of what has been urging me to come this way," Amber informed them, pulsating from bright to dim like a giant, beating heart.

Whether the shifting glow of Amber's form was due to excitement or nervousness, Edward was unsure. "I believe we are ready to go, so if you would please?" Extending his hand, he gestured for the ghostly woman to lead the way.

After traveling for what seemed like half the night, the terrain began to slope gently downward. Amber's pulsating glow started to become more erratic, though none of them had an inkling as to why. Over the course of the last hour, in the sparse light provided by Amber and the moons overhead, they had noticed a couple of minor changes in their surroundings. The normally thick copse of trees around them had begun to thin out slightly, more so, it seemed, the further they trudged forward. The night air, usually cool, felt almost stagnant and oppressive. Without a breeze to stir it, they could feel the humid moisture assaulting their lungs with each breath in the shifting climate. It almost felt like trying to breathe underwater, or perhaps the air of an underground tomb.

"We are getting very close," Amber's whispering voice echoed back to them. Her glowing form had begun to pulsate more rapidly, the way Katie associated with fear. Within moments, the terrain evened out and Amber stopped dead in her tracks.

Following suit, Brian and Katie brought their mechanical horses to a stop. There was a strange, new light emitting from somewhere just ahead. The four of them dismounted and cautiously moved forward. Inching ahead, Edward tapped Brian on the shoulder and whispered in his ear, "Are you sensing anything?"

"I'm getting mixed signals from whatever is in front of us. There is evil present, but not to the degree of anything I would deem as a threat, and my senses tell me there is also something to balance it," he confessed quietly, his tone of voice almost conspiratorial.

Nodding his head, Edward continued forward, pushing low hanging branches from his line of vision. A couple of minutes later, he froze in his tracks. The sight before him was awe inspiring. The forest gave way to what appeared to be a giant meadow, the trees lining it in an enormous circle. What seemed like thousands of tiny blue orbs of light fluttered and swirled through the air about two hundred feet in front of him, some leaving blazing trails of brilliance in their wake. It felt like he was staring into the heavens at a constantly shifting constellation, with a multitude of microscopic comets zipping between the stars.

Slinking up behind Edward, Katie peeked around him at the swirling commotion of light. "Oh my God! It's so beautiful," she whispered in awe.

Acknowledgments

I would like to thank everyone that has helped me with this project. My fiancée, and perhaps my toughest critic, Angela Mullins, for her encouragement, and for putting up with my eccentricities, including my incessant ravings about word count. To Katie Cowan, for once again creating a cover image that was beyond my wildest expectations. To Melissa Ringsted, for doing a fantastic job, as always, with the editing. To my beta readers, Ruthi Kight, Mindy Nabors, Claudine Astbury, Carrie Barringer and Jane Anne Linsdell, for providing their invaluable insight and suggestions. To Mindy Nabors, for her suggestions on the direction of the story. And lastly, to all of my fans and readers. Thank you for buying my book! I hope it brings you as much enjoyment as I got from writing this tale.

Lucian Barnes

From The Tree of Life, the upcoming sixth book in the Desolace Series

Attempting to push past Edward, Katie sighed with frustration when he stuck out an arm to block her path. "I don't think it's a good idea to get any closer. At least, not until daylight when we can see what we're up against," he whispered harshly.

"But—" Katie protested, her eyebrows furrowing and her cheeks puffing out angrily.

"Brian said there was something evil out there," he reminded her. "As much as you may hate me for it, I can't allow you to go blindly rushing toward the lights, no matter how pretty you think they are."

Spinning on her heel, Katie stormed away. Still unsure of what was happening, Julie chased after her.

"I hope her friend can talk some sense into her," Edward commented as the shaman stepped beside him.

"What did you do to piss her off this time?"

"I told her no. Now she's throwing a temper tantrum like a child because I wouldn't allow her to get any closer to that," Edward replied, hitching a thumb toward the swirls of blue light.

Brian nodded his head as Edward spoke, knowing the wizard had likely done the right thing, but wondering about the tactfulness of his wording.

Noting that Amber was no longer nearby, Edward glanced around to locate her. When he saw her floating beside Katie and Julie, he couldn't help but hope the ghost was talking some sense into her.

"Correct me if I'm wrong, but you were wanting to stay here until sunrise, right?" Brian inquired.

"Yes. I want to assess the situation in the light of day," Edward confirmed.

"Can I make a suggestion?"

"By all means," Edward replied, casting a questioning glance toward him.

"We probably still have another few hours of night left. I think it might help relieve a little stress if we start a small campfire and get some rest."

Rubbing his chin thoughtfully, his brows wrinkled in concentration. After considering Brian's proposal for a minute, he let out a soft sigh of resignation. "Perhaps you are right," Edward admitted. "Maybe she is moody because she's tired." His lips stretched out in a thin smile, showing that he, too, was exhausted.

"I think it would be a good idea to get the ball rolling," Brian stated, hearing the heated tone of Katie's voice a short distance from them. With a grim expression, Edward nodded his agreement and they set about the task of gathering firewood. It was a relatively easy task considering that the surrounding trees were dead. They didn't need to search for usable timber; all they had to do was start snapping the low hanging branches from the surrounding, lifeless woods. In no time at all, the two of them managed to gather enough to get them by until daylight.

The crack of breaking limbs distracted Katie from her conversation. Squinting into the near darkness, she realized what the men were doing and exhaled a soft breath of defeat. Since it was obvious that Edward and Brian were preparing to build a fire, she led Julie back to their horse and began removing blankets from its chest cavity. Katie was disappointed that they weren't going to investigate the hazy, blue anomaly right now, but at the same time she was thankful for the opportunity to rest. Although, with all the thoughts bouncing through her head at the moment, she doubted she would get much sleep.

"Are we setting a watch? Relying on my senses? What's the plan?" Brian asked, directing his inquiry to Edward.

"Since Amber is here, I don't think a watch is necessary," he replied, casting a hopeful glance toward the ghostly woman.

Confusion crossed her features momentarily, but she soon felt like she understood the implication. "You want me to watch over everyone?"

"If you would, please. If anything approaches us while we sleep, yell, scream, wail ... do whatever ghosts do to get our attention." He smiled. "Oh, and if we aren't awake when the sky begins to lighten, wake us before you fade."

Despite her belief that slumber would elude her, the warmth of the fire had coaxed Katie into a deep sleep. Once she had entered the coma-like state, Katie was oblivious to the distant cracks and rattles coming from the nearby meadow. Though her companions didn't sleep quite so heavily, their repose was not interrupted by these sounds either. During the night, the noises never grew louder than a faint clatter. Not once did anything approach the sleeping men and women, and not once did Amber attempt to wake them, though she did study the swirling blue dots curiously. She studied the lights so intently that the first rays of dawn rose on the horizon before she realized the sun was starting to rise. Her form had already begun to dissipate, and her vocal cords were useless now. She had no way of waking her friends.

When Katie finally stirred and began her ascension to consciousness, the first light of morning penetrating her closed eyelids, she raised a hand to block the sun's rays. Yawning, she cracked open her eyes and squinted to focus them. The others were still unconscious. Propping herself up on one elbow, Katie turned her gaze toward the meadow and let out a soft gasp. She hadn't known it was there last night, but in the same area she recalled seeing the blue lights there stood the largest tree she had ever seen. Its branches stretched toward the sky like hundreds of slender tentacles, grasping at the clouds overhead. The leaves adorning the limbs appeared huge, even from this distance. Something was hidden amongst the foliage as well, perhaps a fruit of some sort. It was almost what her mind envisioned the fabled tree that Adam and Eve ate from would have looked like. She almost expected a serpent to be writhing within the branches, waiting to tempt anyone who dared get close to the tree with an enormous, polished apple. Even so, she rose to her feet and quietly stepped out of the forest into the sea of withered grass, being careful not to make a sound.

Her boots whispered across the green-brown turf as

she approached the massive, foreign-looking greenery. As she stepped closer and closer, Katie was awed by the size of the enormous trunk supporting the giant tree. By her best estimation, it had to be at least ten feet wide at its base.

Halfway across the meadow, she stopped abruptly. Unless her eyes were playing tricks on her, she had seen something peeking at her from behind the mammoth trunk. Something red, and perhaps taller than human. Suddenly, Katie wasn't sure getting closer was such a good idea. Nervously, she turned her head to gauge the distance she had come, and quickly calculated how long it would take her to reach the safety of the forest and her friends. Letting out a soft sigh through her nose, she slowly spun around to face the strange growth once more.

Curiosity getting the better of her, Katie decided that she *had* to get closer. As she closed the distance, she scanned the branches carefully. Even though the idea was ludicrous, she eyed the limbs with suspicion, as if expecting Adam and Eve's devilish serpent to be staring back at her.

When she was within fifty feet of the massive trunk, Katie realized the tree was even larger than she had first thought. Already, she was standing under the canopy of its branches. Temporarily forgetting about the red shape she had seen moments ago, she swiveled her head to gaze overhead. Blinking her eyes as if she felt she were hallucinating, Katie's mouth gaped open when she realized what she saw was real. Hanging from the limbs were what appeared to be some sort of egg-shaped fruit. There was no uniformity to their size or color, and Katie could see one of the larger egg-fruits undulating.

Mesmerized by the strange, pulsing shapes overhead, Katie was unaware that she was still moving forward. It wasn't until her toes bumped into an obstruction that she looked down. The oddities above her were instantly wiped from her mind. Stretching from the tip of her boots to the trunk of the tree, scattered in a huge circle surrounding it like an obscene mulch, the ground was littered with bones. Human bones. A large, python-like snake slithered across them. Enormous spiders, looking as if they could be distant cousins of the tarantula, wove through the pile spinning their webs and ducking in and out of the eye-holes of skulls. Katie froze in terror, desperate to get away, but scared too much to move, knowing it would attract attention if she did.

Before she could decide what to do, the giant serpent turned its massive head toward her and slowly flicked its long, black tongue, tasting the air to see if the woman was suitable prey. When the reptile continued to slither closer, Katie knew she had to make up her mind quick. She could only hope and pray that her legs would work when she needed them to. Letting out an uneven, frightened breath, she spun around quickly and darted toward the forest, screaming at the top of her lungs.

Made in the USA
Coppell, TX
06 December 2020